P9-CFQ-523

# Just magic.

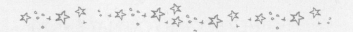

"N ice work," Malik said as Sophie cautiously opened her eyes. She let out a small whoop of excitement as she realized they were in the basement. She quickly uncrossed her legs and shook her limbs to get her circulation going again as she stared around her. Then she clicked her fingers and said, "Visible," before checking herself in the chipped mirror that was hanging up near an old workbench. Apart from the fact that her blonde hair now resembled a bird's nest, she looked the same as she always did. She turned back to Malik and grinned.

"I did it! We flew, we teleported, and we shopped. That's amazing."

"No," Malik said in confusion. "Amazing is the way Jell-O dissolves in your mouth when you eat it. Flying a carpet and teleporting and conjuring up items is just magic."

# OTHER BOOKS YOU MAY ENJOY

The Books of Elsewhere,
Volume 1: *The Shadows*                     Jacqueline West

The Books of Elsewhere,
Volume 2: *Spellbound*                       Jacqueline West

*Eleven*                                     Lauren Myracle

*Gilda Joyce, Psychic Investigator*          Jennifer Allison

Lights, Camera, Cassidy,
Episode 1: *Celebrity*                       Linda Gerber

Lights, Camera, Cassidy,
Episode 2: *Paparazzi*                       Linda Gerber

*Olivia Kidney*                              Ellen Potter

Sophie's Mixed-Up Magic,
Book 1: *Wishful Thinking*                   Amanda Ashby

Sophie's Mixed-Up Magic,
Book 2: *Under a Spell*                      Amanda Ashby

*The Witchy Worries of Abbie Adams*          Rhonda Hayter

# Sophie's
# MIXED-UP
## Magic

## Out of
## Sight

Amanda Ashby

FRANKLIN SQ. PUBLIC LIBRARY
19 LINCOLN ROAD
FRANKLIN SQUARE, N.Y. 11010

BOOK 3

PUFFIN BOOKS
An Imprint of Penguin Group (USA) Inc.

PUFFIN BOOKS

Published by the Penguin Group

Penguin Young Readers Group, 345 Hudson Street, New York, New York 10014, U.S.A.

Penguin Group (Canada), 90 Eglinton Avenue East, Suite 700,
Toronto, Ontario, Canada M4P 2Y3 (a division of Pearson Penguin Canada Inc.)

Penguin Books Ltd, 80 Strand, London WC2R 0RL, England

Penguin Ireland, 25 St Stephen's Green, Dublin 2, Ireland (a division of Penguin Books Ltd)

Penguin Group (Australia), 250 Camberwell Road, Camberwell, Victoria 3124, Australia
(a division of Pearson Australia Group Pty Ltd)

Penguin Books India Pvt Ltd, 11 Community Centre, Panchsheel Park,
New Delhi - 110 017, India

Penguin Group (NZ), 67 Apollo Drive, Rosedale, Auckland 0632, New Zealand
(a division of Pearson New Zealand Ltd)

Penguin Books (South Africa) (Pty) Ltd, 24 Sturdee Avenue,
Rosebank, Johannesburg 2196, South Africa

Registered Offices: Penguin Books Ltd, 80 Strand, London WC2R 0RL, England

Published by Puffin Books, a division of Penguin Young Readers Group, 2012

1 3 5 7 9 10 8 6 4 2

Copyright © Amanda Ashby, 2012
All rights reserved

LIBRARY OF CONGRESS CATALOGING-IN-PUBLICATION DATA IS AVAILABLE
Puffin Books ISBN 978-0-14-241681-5

Printed in the United States of America

All rights reserved. No part of this book may be reproduced, scanned, or distributed
in any printed or electronic form without permission. Please do not participate in or encourage
piracy of copyrighted materials in violation of the author's rights. Purchase only authorized editions.

## Acknowledgments

Once again I need to thank all of the usual suspects. Jenny Bent, Karen Chaplin, Kristin Gilson, Sara Hantz, and Christina Phillips. This book wouldn't exist without you—though I'm really not sure you should be encouraging a grown woman to write about a Cheetos-addicted ghost!

A big shout out to all my colleagues and customers at Napier Library, with special thanks to Mark, Caleb, Maryanne, Katrina, Jamie, and Milla, who were always happy to talk about very strange plot scenarios at the drop of a hat. I miss you all.

Also, thanks to everyone at Puffin for their continued support, and to all the bloggers, teachers, librarians and booksellers who have introduced readers to my strange little world!

# 1

**S**OLOMON'S ELIXIR.

Sophie Campbell's fingers tightened around the tiny vial of amber liquid, which shimmered and sparkled like the sun rising over the Sahara Desert. Well, okay, so Sophie hadn't ever seen the sun rising over the Sahara Desert, but Malik, her ghostly djinn guide, had assured her that it was completely identical, minus all the locusts. Not that it really mattered what the liquid looked like; the important thing was that it was not only the most sought-after magic in the djinn kingdom, but it was also the key to freeing her father from the binds of Sheterum, an evil sahir. The idea made Sophie feel giddy, because the sooner her dad was freed, the sooner they could be a proper family again.

Her smile faded slightly.

Unfortunately, there was one small chink in her very good plan. In order for the elixir to free her father, she needed to find out where he was being held, and that was proving to be a problem. A big problem. Thankfully, Sophie was a positive person, and she was sure that the

Universe wouldn't have helped her find all of the ingredients to make the elixir (including eel-tail-oil extract, which, for the record, stank worse than gym socks) if it wasn't going to help her find out where her father was.

And so Sophie slipped the precious vial back into the pocket of her jeans as she made her way through the crowded backstage area of the Robert Robertson Middle School auditorium on Monday afternoon.

"Sorry, I'm late," she puffed as she came to a halt alongside her two best friends, who were standing next to a papier-mâché flying monkey called Colin. Sophie widened her eyes. "Wow, he looks amazing."

"I know, right?" Kara agreed as she flipped a strand of long dark hair out of her face and carefully inspected one of the wings to make sure it was okay. Kara, who was the artist of the trio, had spent the last couple of weeks up to her elbows in glue and newspaper making props for the upcoming musical, *The Wizard of Oz*.

"Well, I just hope that they're using lots of ropes on him, because if he falls, someone is going to get seriously splattered. I saw this movie once where that exact thing happened," Harvey, the movie buff of the three, said as he knit his brows together.

"Colin isn't going to be splattering anyone," Kara cut him off before he could talk about anything too gruesome. Then she turned back to Sophie and wrinkled her nose. "Anyway, where have you been? The dress rehearsal starts in five minutes. I was beginning to think that you'd forgotten about it."

"Of course I didn't forget about it." Sophie looked horrified as she wiped the sweat away from her brow and silently concluded that if she had to keep running around school like this, she was going to have to get a lot fitter. "You know that I would never let you down like that."

"Well, that's good." Kara looked relieved as she fiddled with one of Colin's monkey ears. "I'm so nervous about Colin's big day."

"She's not exaggerating," Harvey confirmed as he held out his arm. "She's been pinching me for the last ten minutes to help her calm down. I'm sure I'm going to have a bruise tomorrow. So what happened? Did you get distracted by Jonathan?"

At the mention of Jonathan Tait's name, Sophie let out a happy sigh, since she thought the seventh grader, with his tanned skin and blond hair, was the most perfect guy in the whole entire world. Plus, he loved Neanderthal Joe almost as much as Sophie did, and they had sortofkindofmaybe been hanging out together ever since she had started sixth grade last month. Then she realized her two friends were looking at her expectantly, so she lost the dreamy expression and gave a quick shake of her head.

"No, it didn't have anything to do with Jonathan," she assured them. "It's just that on my way here I noticed that the cafeteria was serving meat loaf."

"Meat loaf?" Kara squeaked, her normally relaxed face suddenly looking far from happy. "You nearly missed Colin's first proper rehearsal because of some meat loaf?"

"Well, in Sophie's defense, the cafeteria here does make very good meat loaf," Harvey offered. "Much better than what we got at Miller Road Elementary, that's for sure. Apparently, they've got a special secret. *What?*" he protested as he suddenly realized the two girls were staring at him. "It's true."

"We believe you," Sophie quickly assured him before she turned back to Kara, who was glancing nervously around the backstage area. "But what I mean is that I've been looking for Malik. He promised he would be here by now, so when I saw that the cafeteria was doing meat loaf, I thought he might've snuck in there to steal some."

Her friends both nodded knowingly—stealing meat loaf from the cafeteria was exactly the sort of thing that Malik was likely to do. Unfortunately, ever since Sophie herself had become a djinn, she had been stuck with him as her djinn guide. Not that he did much guiding. Instead, he spent most of his time watching YouTube clips, eating Cheetos, and getting Sophie into trouble. Usually all at the same time. Unfortunately, he was also the only hope she had of finding out where her father was.

"So I gather that Malik wasn't there," Kara said, her voice full of understanding.

"No." Sophie let out a frustrated sigh. "I even checked

behind the deep fryer, where they were cooking the meat loaf, but there was no sign of him."

"Ah, so that's the secret to the meat loaf. Deep-frying. Nice." Harvey, who was a big fan of eating, nodded his head in approval before he realized they were staring at him again, and so he coughed. "*But so not the point.* Have you tried clapping him?"

"I've been clapping him all morning," Sophie said, since according to Malik, clapping was like ringing a doorbell, and when she did it he would appear. However, if this was true, then all she could conclude was that Malik's doorbell was broken. Very, very broken. "What if something's happened to him? What if—"

Before she could finish, Patrick Dutton, an emo-looking seventh grader with aqua eyes and Justin Bieber hair, strode toward them. He had a clipboard in one hand and what looked like part of the yellow brick road in the other. Kara immediately started to blush.

"Hey, Kara. The rehearsal is just about to start, but you can watch it from the front. And don't worry, I'll take good care of Colin for you," Patrick said with a wink. But instead of replying, Kara began to fiddle with her hair as she mumbled something that sounded very much like *mwhooahwwh*. Then, as Patrick carefully moved Colin over to the left side of the stage, Kara dropped her head and hurried to the front of the auditorium as fast as her long legs would take her. Sophie and Harvey exchanged a surprised glance before they raced after her.

"Um, excuse me, what's going on?" Sophie demanded as she finally caught up with her friend and they all sat down in an empty row of seats.

"Nothing. Nothing's going on," Kara said in a rush, and shot Sophie a concerned look.

"So why were you acting so—" Sophie started to say, her eyes widening. "Kara, do you have a crush on Patrick?"

"What?" Kara blinked as she studied her fingers, refusing to look up at either of her friends. "No, of course not. W-why would you think I had a crush on him? That's crazy talk."

"Er, because you did *this* and *this* when he was talking to you," Sophie said as she tugged at her hair to demonstrate Kara's nervous behavior. "Not to mention the whole *mwhooahwwh* thing. Is that even a word?"

"Oh no." Kara let out a long groan as her cheeks turned the color of ketchup. "So do you think that he noticed?"

"Only if he had ears and eyes," Harvey assured her. Sophie hit him in the arm.

"Of course he didn't, and the only reason we noticed was because we know you so well," Sophie quickly reassured her as she realized that Kara *did* have a crush on Patrick. Why hadn't Kara told her? But she already knew the answer. She had been so caught up with finding her dad and the whole djinn thing that she hadn't realized Kara even knew Patrick, let alone had a crush on him. She was a bad friend. "So why didn't you tell us you liked him?"

"At first I didn't know I liked him. He's one of the stage-hands, and he's been coming to the art room to check on Colin's progress," Kara explained as she nervously fiddled with her necklace. "And that's when I noticed the color of his eyes. I mean, did you see them? They were like the ocean on a summer's day with just a hint of lapis in there." She let out a dreamy sigh, and her shoulders started to droop. "But of course it's hopeless. You saw me. I can't even string two words together when I'm around him. Why would he ever like me?"

"Um, because you are gorgeous, not to mention sweet, kind, and funny. Oh, and you're also very nice to papier-mâché flying monkeys," Sophie said. "And if you like him, then you should do something about it."

"W-well, he did tell me that the whole drama club is going to see *The Wizard of Oz* at the movies on Saturday for inspiration. It's a sing-along. Anyway, he kind of asked me to go with them," Kara reluctantly admitted.

"He did not." Sophie widened her eyes as she gripped her friend's arm in excitement. "That's so majorly excit-ing!"

"Yeah, the thing is that I'm not so sure it would be a good idea." Kara shook her head. "What if I get all tongue-tied again and I'm stuck there on my own? I wish I could be more like you when you're around Jonathan. How do you manage to speak to him without feeling like you're going to melt into a puddle?"

"I don't know," Sophie said truthfully as she considered it. "I guess I'm always so excited to see him, and then we're normally so busy talking about Neanderthal Joe that there's no time to be nervous. Perhaps you just need to make sure you talk about things you're interested in?"

"I guess." Kara still didn't look convinced, and Sophie felt another pang of guilt that she hadn't been more helpful to her friend. Then she had an idea.

"Hey, what if Harvey and I went with you? I mean, I know that we're technically not part of the drama club, but it's a public movie theater, so there's nothing to stop us from going, too," Sophie said, and Kara immediately brightened.

"Really? You guys would do that?"

"Actually." Harvey coughed. "I can't. My mom's making me go along to some lame single-parent camp next weekend so we can bond with other single-parent families."

"Oh, Harvey, that's terrible." Sophie shot him a sympathetic look. His parents had recently split up, and he was now caught right in the middle of all the warring.

"Tell me about it. I swear that my mom's only doing it to bug my dad because he wanted me to go to the lake with him. Honestly, parents are so complicated."

"So are they talking to each other yet?" Kara looked worried, and Harvey shook his head, his long bangs swaying back and forth.

"Not exactly, though they are talking *about* each other

a lot. Mainly to me, so now I just put my earbuds in and nod from time to time. Something that I plan on doing the whole weekend while I'm away at Camp Touchy-Feely," he said as he blew his hair out of his eyes.

"Maybe it's a sign that I shouldn't go to the movie?" Kara said immediately, her pale green eyes full of worry. Sophie shook her head. "You have to go. And even though Harvey can't make it, you've still got me. Oh, and we should get you a new outfit. You could ask your mom to take us to the mall. You know how excited she gets when you want to exchange your paint-splattered wardrobe for something new," Sophie said. Of course she would've been happy to conjure something up, but Kara's mom had a bad habit of noticing new clothes and wondering where they had come from.

"What? Oh please, not more crushes. I mean, first we had all the business with Sophie and Jonathan Tait, and now Kara likes someone? Honestly, I don't know where you kids ever get the time to just do your homework," a voice suddenly said. They all looked up to where Malik—Sophie's djinn guide—was now floating in front of them, a frown on his face.

Today he was wearing a bright yellow Hawaiian shirt and some skinny jeans, and his Zac Efron hair was slicked back away from his face. He also had a bulky man bag slung over his shoulder, which he refused to stop using, despite Sophie's assertion that it was the ugliest thing in the entire world. Thankfully, because he was a ghost,

Sophie and her friends were the only ones who could see him. It was a small comfort.

"Malik, you're finally back. This waiting has been driving me crazy," she said, deciding that it was easiest just to ignore his earlier comments. Instead, she took a deep breath and braced herself. "So? Did you find anything out?"

"As a matter of fact, I did," Malik announced with a flourish of his arms. "I discovered that—*burning sand dunes, what is that noise?* Is someone being tortured? I thought that kind of thing was frowned upon in middle school."

"Don't be rude. It's the dress rehearsal for *The Wizard of Oz*. She doesn't sound *that* bad," Kara protested as they looked over at the stage, where Claudia Rodgers, who was playing Dorothy, was starting to sing "Somewhere Over the Rainbow."

"I beg to differ." Malik shuddered as Claudia made a wobbly key change. "I knew I should've gone to the last audition, because they obviously needed the help of an expert to do their casting."

"Since when are you an expert?" Harvey raised an eyebrow.

"Hello, I've watched *High School Musical* over three hundred times, not to mention the fact that I'm the spitting image of Zac Efron, which I think you'll agree makes me very qualified. And that, my friends, is not music. I'm pretty sure that noise like that is illegal in several states and—"

"Malik," Sophie cut him off again as she clutched her hands together and tried to ignore the way her heart was pounding. "What did you find out?"

"Huh?" He blinked for a minute before realizing what he had been talking about. "Oh yes, sorry. I got distracted by that girl's dreadful wailing. But as I was saying, I, Malik the Great, djinn guide extraordinaire and all-around fantastic ghost, have discovered where Sheterum is holding Sophie's father."

ARE YOU SERIOUS? HAVE YOU REALLY FOUND HIM?"
Harvey asked, but Sophie hardly heard. She couldn't
even hear the horrible singing in the background. All she
was conscious of was the fact that her heart was beating
at a million miles an hour as Malik's words rang out over
and over again in her mind. He had found her dad.

*Her dad.*

Excitement and joy raced through her in equal mea-
sures. This was something that she had dreamed and
hoped for ever since her dad had walked out on them almost four years ago. Of course, at the time she thought the
reason he hadn't come home was because he had amnesia
or had been abducted by aliens, not because he was a djinn
who was bound to an evil sahir. But that was beside the
point. The point was, all her positive thinking had paid off.

And soon he would be at home and they would once
again be a regular family.

"Of course I've really found him." Malik looked at
Harvey in confusion. "Why would I say that I have if I

haven't? You know, I just don't understand you kids some-times."

"Um, because that's the sort of thing you usually do," Harvey replied.

"Name one time."

"Only one?" Harvey asked as he held up his fingers. "Well, let's see. There was that time you told Sophie that—"

"Hey, can we stop with the bickering?" Kara admonished them both and turned to Sophie, a concerned expression on her face. "Are you okay? You haven't said anything yet."

"I-I'm fine." Sophie slowly nodded; she felt her heartbeat return to normal as she turned to Malik. "It was just a lot to take in, but I'm okay. So Malik, tell us everything. What happened? Where is he? More importantly, how soon can we go and rescue him? Oh, and can I get a message to him?"

"No message, definitely not." Malik shook his head. "Because, trust me, the less Sheterum knows about you, the better. Now, if you will stop interrupting, I will tell you what happened and we can get out of here before that girl starts to murder any more songs," he said, glaring at the stage.

"Sorry." Sophie nodded for him to continue. Malik adjusted his shirt and rolled his shoulders before waving his hand with a flourish.

"Okay, so for the last few days I kept hearing about

this djinn called Manny the Moody, who was allegedly bound to Sheterum before getting freed last year. So I decided to track him down. Unfortunately, it's not as easy to hunt out low-life double-dealing djinns as it once was." Then he paused and let out a nostalgic sigh. "You know, I remember a time when every djinn worth his weight in smokeless fire would be at the camel races, throwing back date juice like there was no tomorrow and gambling with stolen money. But seriously, when I went there today, it was almost deserted. I blame the Internet, because—"

"Malik." Harvey coughed to get him back on track.

"All right. Keep your overgrown hair on," Malik muttered. "So anyway, while I didn't find Manny, I did find Karl the Kleptomaniac. I haven't seen him in ages, and while he's probably the worst thief I've ever seen, he does love to gossip, and for three hamburgers and some curly fries he sang like a canary. He told me that Manny managed to break his bind by doing some morally questionable things involving art theft. Apparently, Sheterum fancies himself as the next big collector, and the djinns who help him the most are the ones who earn back their freedom the fastest."

"He makes them steal artwork?" Kara, who had been intently staring at the corner of the stage where Patrick was adjusting a microphone lead, suddenly burst out. "That's unbelievable."

"My dad would never do that." Sophie quickly shook her head. "Ever."

"Yes, from everything I've heard about Tariq, I'm afraid you're right," Malik agreed, as if her father's refusal to steal was a bad thing. "Which is why it's lucky for him that we really did manage to brew Solomon's Elixir, or else he would probably be stuck there forever."

"Malik, I don't think you're helping," Kara scolded him while Sophie felt sick at the prospect.

"Hey, I'm not judging. To each his own, that's what I say," Malik assured her in a serene voice.

"So what now?" Sophie asked, as a ripple of impatience went racing through her. "When can we go and free my dad? Can we do it after school?"

"Sure. As long as you have floor plans highlighting Sheterum's state-of-the-art security system so you can avoid all of his booby traps—which, for the record, normally involve flying discs that sever your spinal cord," Malik said mildy. "Since, in case you haven't figured it out yet, sahirs aren't just evil, they are paranoid as well, and Sheterum is the most paranoid of them all. Not to mention a total hermit who hardly ever leaves his mansion."

"What?" Kara yelped in alarm. "So what are you saying? That Sophie won't be able to rescue her dad?"

"No, Miss Glass Is Half Empty, I'm not saying that at all, I'm just saying that we need to wait until Sheterum does leave his mansion. Thankfully, Sophie's positive thinking has paid off because look at this." As he spoke he pulled a gilt-trimmed brochure out of his ugly man bag and passed it over.

"What is it?" Sophie asked as she studied it, desperately trying to remind herself that she was a positive person who had no time for negative thoughts.

"It's an invitation to an auction of postmodern art," Kara said as she leaned over Sophie's shoulder to read it. Then she looked back up at Malik in surprise. "Since when do you like postmodern art?"

"I don't." Malik shuddered. "I'm a simple djinn with simple tastes. I mean, what's so wrong with an apple looking like an apple? Or a singer who can sing," he added as he again glared at the stage, where Claudia was now attempting "We're Off to See the Wizard."

"But what's it got to do with Sophie's dad?" Kara's brows knitted together.

Before Malik could answer, Harvey widened his eyes. "Hey, I see where you're going with this! If Sheterum is at the art auction, then he won't be in his house, and that will be the best time to go rescue Sophie's dad."

"Exactly." Malik clapped his hands in approval, but Sophie felt her throat tighten as she studied the date.

"A week from Friday? I can't possibly wait that long. There must be something we can do to rescue my dad sooner," she pleaded. But Malik shook his head.

"No. Haven't I just explained why we need to wait? Besides, I still need to track down Manny and convince him—in a kind and completely noninvasive, highly ethical way—to tell me all the details about Sheterum's security system."

"And what if you can't find him in time?" Harvey softly asked the question that everyone was thinking.

"Harvey's right. Is there some kind of backup plan?" Kara asked, concern written all over her face. "Perhaps you could ask Rufus?"

"Ask Rufus?" Malik stared at them all like they had just asked him to rap dance. Then he turned to Sophie and folded his arms. "Can you please explain to your friends what the first rule of being a djinn is?"

"Never play poker with another djinn," Sophie dutifully repeated, not really sure what he was getting at.

"Exactly," Malik agreed with a nod of his head. "And the reason we have that rule is because other djinns are liars, cheats, and scoundrels. And despite the fact I've known Rufus for many centuries, let me assure you that I wouldn't trust that orange, overweight, smooth-talking dirtbag any farther than I could throw him. In fact, out of all the lying, cheating scoundrels, Rufus is the worst."

"But why can't he help?" Now it was Kara's turn to look confused.

"Because apart from being completely untrustworthy, he is deceptively clever and shrewd, and if he knows for a second that Sophie is looking for her father, he will quickly realize that she must've figured out how to make Solomon's Elixir, since that's the only way Tariq can possibly be freed. And trust me, if Rufus suspects that Sophie has the elixir, the rest won't bear thinking about. Which is why discretion is so important here. Are we clear?"

"Yes," they all murmured at once.

"And besides," Malik added as he reached into his man bag and pulled out a second brochure. "You're going to have plenty of things to keep you busy."

"Like what?" Sophie asked in a cautious voice as she took the brochure from him and blinked. It appeared to be about a carpet sale.

"Well, you see, there is one other teeny, tiny thing that I forgot to mention earlier. Turns out that Sheterum doesn't live in San Francisco. He lives in Los Angeles, and if Sophie wants to rescue her dad, she's going to have to learn how to fly."

"I STILL CAN'T BELIEVE THAT YOU'RE GOING TO learn to fly on a carpet," Harvey said for the hundredth time as the final bell rang and they made their way across the parking lot to the school-bus stop. "I mean, you're going to fly. Properly fly in the sky. Do you have any idea how amazing that is?"

"It is pretty cool." Sophie suppressed a smile as she watched Harvey pretend to surf along the gravel path. Then she took another peek at the catalogue Malik had given her. She had ended up selecting a purple-and-red-patterned carpet. Malik had looked faintly disgusted by her choice, but all the same he had gone off to order it for her. He was also going to start making discreet inquiries about Manny (not that the words *Malik* and *discreet* normally went together).

"So, do you think that once you've mastered it, you'll be able to take me up for a spin?" Harvey demanded as he put out his arms and almost knocked a passing ninth grader in the nose. He quickly dropped his hands back down by his sides and looked contrite.

"I don't know, I'll have to ask Malik, but if he doesn't mind, then I don't," Sophie said, still in a daze over everything that had happened.

"Nice." Harvey nodded his head in approval before turning to Kara, who was walking beside them. "Don't you agree, K?"

"Um, sure." Kara slowly nodded her head, but it was obvious that she wasn't very happy. Sophie immediately came to a halt and stared at her friend in concern.

"Are you okay? Are you worried about Patrick or the stagehand dropping Colin on his head? Remember, we checked him, and he was fine."

"No, it's not that." Kara shook her long hair and let out a reluctant sigh. "Look, I know how excited you are about finding your dad, but the thing is, you're talking about flying on a carpet to Los Angeles. I mean, that's pretty intense, considering that we're not even allowed to go to the mall on our own."

"Yes, but that's because lunatics hang out at the mall," Harvey pointed out, obviously alarmed that Kara's concern might stop Sophie from wanting to try it. "Whereas I'm pretty sure that Sophie's carpet will be lunatic-free."

"I know." Kara gave a solemn nod. "But I'm just not sure about this. I wonder if you should tell your mom."

For a moment Sophie was quiet. "Trust me, it's something I've been thinking about a lot. But what if she doesn't believe me? Or worse, what if she grounds me? Then I might miss this chance, and my dad will be there for even longer. Plus, while you were making sure that Colin really hadn't been damaged, Malik told me that once I master my normal carpet-flying abilities, I should be able to just use it like a teleporter, so I won't actually be flying for hours in the sky, I'll be jumping from one location to another. So in a way it will just be like going next door."

"Okay, now you're going to teleport?" Harvey's jaw dropped, but the two girls ignored him as a look of relief washed over Kara's face.

"I didn't know that. S-so does Malik really think you will be able to learn everything in time?"

"Well, he did say that it only took him a week to learn. But then he added that he was a djinn of exceptional talent," Sophie told her. "But I just know that I'll be able to. I have to be able to, because the idea of my dad being bound by such a hideous creature is unbearable. But I promise I'll be careful. Plus, Malik will be with me the whole time. I've been waiting to find my dad for so long, I'm just really scared of doing anything that will stop me from finding him. Does that even make sense?"

"Yes." Kara finally spoke as they started to walk again. "It does. And I didn't mean to sound unsupportive, I was just worried. Especially since, as well as its being so far away, it's a lot to juggle."

"Lucky I've become an expert juggler since Malik

came into my life," Sophie reminded her, and Kara nodded.

"Good point. You've got to do whatever it takes to get your dad home, and if you can face the smell of the cafeteria to look for Malik, then you can face this. I shouldn't have even said anything."

"Of course you should've," Sophie assured her as she gave Kara's hand a squeeze and Harvey made a groaning noise.

"Is this going to be one of those times when you both get all girly, because I'm telling you now that I'm not doing a group hug." Harvey folded his arms tightly around his skinny chest.

"It's okay, Harvey. No group hug," Kara assured him with a watery smile. Then she gave Sophie a nudge. "Hey, look who is waiting for you."

"Who?" Sophie started to say before she glanced over to where Jonathan Tait was looking all kinds of gorgeous as he leaned against one of the large ornamental boulders that sat outside the school.

Today he was wearing a Neanderthal Joe concert T-shirt and his favorite baggy Levi's, which had a little rip in the back pocket. Even better, the minute he saw her, he started to grin. Sophie's stomach flipped, and she paused for a second and wished for her superstraight hair to have a bit more bounce in it.

Jonathan was someone else whom she longed to tell about her new powers, but she had promised Malik that for now she would keep them a secret. So instead, she gave her newly bouncy hair a quick pat and arranged to meet her friends at the bus stop before she made her way toward him. First all the good news about her dad and now seeing Jonathan. This day was getting better by the minute.

"Soph," Jonathan said as he stopped reading his text messages and quickly thrust his cell phone back into the pocket of his jeans. "I was hoping I would catch you before you left. I was looking for you at lunchtime, but I couldn't find you anywhere."

"You were?" Sophie asked in a dreamy voice, not quite able to hide her goofy grin. "If I'd known that, I wouldn't have spent so much time with Colin," she said, before suddenly worrying that he might think she meant Colin Templeton, who was a seventh-grade chess genius and a part-time nose picker. "I mean Colin the flying monkey—well, his name isn't really Colin—that's just what Kara calls him. She helped make him. He's in the school musical."

Jonathan immediately shook his head and grinned. "Well, I'm glad you weren't hanging out with Colin Templeton, because when I sat next to him in bio this morning, it smelled like he hadn't had a shower in a week," Jonathan said, and Sophie's smile grew wider. "I should've looked in the auditorium," he continued. "I walked past there, too, but the noise scared me. Not quite the same as a Neanderthal Joe concert."

"Not even close." She gave an adamant shake of her head. She and her friends had gone to the recent Neanderthal Joe concert with Jonathan and his older brother, and if that wasn't blissful enough, they had even managed to go backstage, where Eddie Henry (Best Bass Player in the World) had given Sophie his guitar pick. It was also where she and Jonathan had accidently touched hands and totally *had a moment*.

"So anyway, the thing is, I kind of wanted to ask you something, and since I've got a basketball tournament all day tomorrow, I really need to do it today." Jonathan gave an awkward cough, which abruptly caused Sophie to stop her reminiscing.

"Really?" Sophie's heart pounded in excitement, but before he could say anything else, his cell phone started to beep. Instead of answering it, he let out a long groan.

"Sorry about that. It's my sister. She's having a major meltdown because there are no books left in the library for her to do her assignment on the fall of the Roman Empire, and now she wants me to help her. Like it's my fault she went shoe shopping and had a three-day *Twilight* movie marathon. Anyway, now she's annoyed because I wanted to come and find you instead of staying with her."

"Y-you told her that you would rather see me?" Sophie asked in a cautious voice, since, because of a couple of small misunderstandings involving a pair of jeans and, more recently, Melissa's boyfriend, Ben Griggs, Jonathan's twin sister wasn't Sophie's biggest fan. They had recently reached a kind of understanding, but Sophie didn't have much faith that it would last for long.

"Three times," Jonathan assured her as his cell phone started to beep once again. Then he shrugged. "Unfortunately, she's not very good at not getting her own way."

Yup, that was something Sophie knew only too well. She also knew that not only would Melissa probably blame Sophie for this, but she would also keep texting and texting, and then Sophie would never find out what Jonathan wanted to ask her before the bus arrived.

Sophie let out a reluctant sigh and reminded herself that as a positive person she should enjoy helping people. Even evil people like Melissa Tait. So she closed her eyes for a second and wished that a whole heap of Roman history books would appear at the library. Then, after she felt the familiar tingle, she opened her eyes and turned back to Jonathan.

"Tell her to go to the back of the nonfiction section. Right by the far window there's a half-empty shelf. I'm sure she'll find everything she needs there."

"What? Are you serious?" Jonathan looked surprised. "I was talking to the librarian yesterday, and she said that every single book on the Roman Empire was checked out. I wonder why she didn't mention those?"

*Er, that would be because I've only just magically conjured them up.* However, since she couldn't exactly admit that to

Jonathan, she just gave a vague shrug. "I don't know, but history is my favorite subject, which is how I found them. It's kind of like a secret stash."

"Well, thanks. It's really nice of you to help her like this. I can't say she deserves it, but I'll tell her what you said," Jonathan assured her. He pulled his cell phone out, and his fingers flew across the keyboard, but instead of a rapid response, there was nothing. After a few more moments he shot her an apologetic look.

"No reply?" Sophie asked in a nervous voice, suddenly wondering whether she had messed up the wish. It was entirely possible. Especially since she had never wished for something to appear in a separate location before. Then she let out a long groan as she realized that now Melissa might think that Sophie had told her about the books just to waste her time.

What was it with her and her ability to annoy Jonathan's twin sister? Why hadn't she just stayed out of it? After all, it wasn't her fault that Melissa hadn't done her assignment, but now Melissa would probably twist it around and blame Sophie.

"I'm sorry about that. I guess the books weren't there, but she could've at least said thanks to you for trying to help her." Jonathan looked embarrassed but not surprised. "Anyway, at least she's stopped interrupting us," he said in a brighter voice as he pocketed his cell phone.

"That's true," Sophie agreed, wishing she could share his confidence. However, since there wasn't much she could do about it now, she looked at him shyly. "S-so you were going to ask me something?"

"What?" He blinked for a moment before dropping his head and fidgeting with his fingers. Harvey was going to have a field day with the body language. "Oh yeah. But if it sounds too dumb, or you, you know, you'd rather stay in and watch TV, then that's totally cool, because—"

"Rather than do what?" Sophie knitted her eyebrows together in confusion.

He let out a sigh. "Rather than come to my folks' anniversary party. They're having a big fancy thing in two weeks. It's on a Sunday afternoon, and they said I could bring someone. It's probably going to be lame. I mean, who has anniversary parties anymore? Who even has parents who are married anymore, and—"

"I think it's cool that your parents are still together," Sophie cut him off, causing Jonathan to wince.

"Oh, hey, sorry, I didn't mean to rub it in that your dad isn't around. You must think that I'm the biggest idiot."

"Of course I don't," Sophie quickly reassured him, not least since she was planning on having her dad back very soon. "I think it's really nice that your parents want to celebrate. And I would love to come. I mean, I have to check with my mom first, but if she says it's okay, then—"

"Really?" Jonathan's dark brown eyes widened, and a look of relief spread across his face. "Wow, okay, well, that's great. Oh and here, you'd better take this so your mom can see that it's all official." As he spoke, he pulled a fancy invitation out of his back pocket and handed it to her.

"Thanks." Sophie felt a goofy smile make its way onto her face.

"No worries. Anyway, I'd better go and stop my sister from failing yet another assignment," he said as he jogged away, leaving Sophie with the goofy smile still in place. Not only was he funny and gorgeous, but he was nice to his evil sister. He really was perfect. And he wanted her to meet his parents. The idea made her feel weak with happiness. The minute he was gone she hurried over to where the bus was pulling up.

"So?" Kara instantly demanded as they piled onto the bus. "What was that all about? Harvey said that Jonathan was looking really nervous and uncomfortable. He wasn't telling you that he had rabies or something, was he?"

"Definitely no rabies," Sophie assured her friends as they grabbed seats near the middle of the bus. "He was actually inviting me to his parents' anniversary party next month."

"No way." Kara grinned before widening her eyes. "Oh, and that means you can wear—"

"I know. Can you believe it?" Sophie immediately squealed as Harvey looked at them both blankly.

"Believe what?" he demanded. "You know I hate it when you two do that mind-reading thing. What's going on?"

"Sorry, Harvey," Kara immediately apologized. "It's

just, when we were at the mall the other day, Sophie tried on the most amazing outfit. It was a floral dress—"

"With a totally cute shrug to go with it," Sophie butted in with a grin as she closed her eyes and wished for a picture of the outfit to appear. A second later it was in her hand, and she passed it over to him. "See, isn't it adorable?"

"Yes, very adorable," he said in an obedient voice as he rolled his eyes, but the two girls, who were used to him, just ignored it.

"Trust me, it's going to be perfect," Kara assured her. "That must've been the party that I heard Melissa and her Tait-bots talking about yesterday."

At the mention of Jonathan's sister, Sophie recalled her latest faux pas and felt her mood dip. "Well, hopefully it will be so massive that Melissa won't notice that I'm there."

"But I thought you two had sorted things out." Now it was Kara's turn to look confused.

"I know," Sophie agreed as she told her friends about what had happened. When she was finished, Kara let out a long groan while Harvey stared at her in disbelief.

"Okay so are you saying that you magically tried to give her some history books to stop her from texting Jonathan so much? Did you learn *nothing* from what happened last time you tried to be nice to Melissa Tait?" Harvey demanded, reminding her that a couple of weeks ago, in order to become friends with Melissa, Sophie had decided to use her djinn powers to join the cheerleading squad. Instead, she had accidently given Melissa her djinn ring and, in the process, ended up being bound to her—and forced to respond to Melissa's every wish. Not exactly an experience that she was keen to repeat in a hurry.

"I know," Sophie acknowledged as she subconsciously wrapped her fingers around the large rhinestone-encrusted apple-shaped ring to double-check it was still there. Once bound, twice shy, and all of that. Then she realized her friends were both looking at her. She coughed. "Anyway, now she's going to blame me for making Jonathan late to help her and because I told her to go and find some books that weren't there. What am I going to do?"

"Cross your fingers and hope that she doesn't fail her assignment and take another vendetta out against you," Harvey suggested in an apologetic voice. "There isn't much else you can do. Are you sure you can't wipe her mind and make her forget?"

Sophie shook her head. Unfortunately, her powers extended only to conjuring up physical items; she wasn't able to change the way someone else acted or behaved. Which was a pity really.

"I'm sure it will be fine," Kara added in an encouraging voice.

"I hope so," Sophie agreed as the bus went over a bump and they all bounced up in the air. "It's just so annoying that Jonathan's twin sister has to be the most evil girl in the whole entire world." Then she brightened as she looked at the invitation again. One Tait might not like her, but another did. Now that she had the outfit, all she needed was the perfect present. What was the perfect present for someone's parents? However, before she could give it any more thought, the school bus trundled to a halt, and Sophie hopped off the bus, waved good-bye to her friends, and hurried up to her two-story weatherboard house.

It was looking a bit worse for wear, with its peeling paint and overgrown lawn, but for once Sophie didn't mind because very soon her dad would be back home and the house would finally be restored to its former glory.

She grinned as she hurried into the kitchen, where her mom was surrounded by pieces of paper and Meg was staring into the fridge, as if willing something to appear.

"How was your day?" Her mom looked up from her papers.

Sophie automatically smiled. "You're not going to believe this, but Jonathan invited me to go to his parents' anniversary party. It's in two weeks, on a Sunday afternoon at their house. Please say I can go. Please, please, please."

"A party? I want to go, too," Meg immediately announced as she shut the fridge door and hurried over.

"Well you can't," Sophie retorted. While Meg looked like an angel with blonde curls and big blue eyes, she was actually obsessed with sharks and would no doubt spend the whole party grossing everyone out with stories of how a human leg had once been found in the belly of a great white.

"Yes, but I want to go. Jonathan told me that his dad went scuba diving with a shark, but when I asked him if anyone got eaten, Jonathan didn't know. So I need to talk to his dad about it." Meg pouted. *See.*

"And maybe you can ask him that one day," their mom said in a mild voice as she pushed a strand of blonde hair, so similar to Sophie's own, away from her face. "But it won't be at the party."

"Why not?" Meg demanded as her lower lip started to poke out. "Why should everyone else get to go out and do cool stuff? I want to do something, too."

"Meg," their mom warned, and Sophie's sister finally shut her mouth.

"Thanks." Sophie mentally wiped her brow before her fingers curled around the Eddie Henry guitar pick, which was hanging around her neck. It wasn't magical, but she still loved holding it. "So may I go? Please, Mom? Jonathan said that you can call his mom and check with her, plus I even have my own invitation. See?" She pulled it out of her pocket and handed it over.

"Actually," her mom admitted as she smoothed down the invitation and grinned. "I've already talked to Monica Tait about it. She ordered some of my pottery for her art gallery and I just delivered it today."

"What?" Sophie was immediately distracted as she

wrinkled her nose. "Mrs. Tait bought some of your pottery for her art gallery? Why didn't I know about this?"

"You did, but I think I made the mistake of telling you when Jonathan had just sent you an e-mail using three smiley faces on it."

Sophie paused for a moment and grinned. That had been a particularly adorable message. If her mom had been talking then, there was a good chance Sophie *hadn't* been listening.

"That's right, you were drooling," Meg informed her in a helpful voice, but Sophie ignored her as she turned to her mom.

"So what about the party? Does this mean I can go?" she asked as she continued to clutch at the guitar pick around her neck.

"Yes, it means you can go," her mom said, a smile hovering across her lips.

"That's so unfair," Meg grumbled, but Sophie hardly heard as she hurried upstairs, since she now had an outfit to plan, a carpet to learn to fly, and her homework to do. She was pretty sure that life didn't get any better.

4

"OKAY," MALIK ANNOUNCED HALF AN HOUR LATER as he floated around Sophie's bedroom. "When it comes to flying a carpet, there are three very important things to remember. Can you tell me what they are?"

"Malik, do we really need to do this?" Sophie let out a soft groan and studied the sheet of paper that Malik had given her when they'd first started. And to think that she had been looking forward to this.

"Well I don't need to because I'm awesome and I already know how to fly a carpet, but since you're a noob who has never even hovered off the ground before, you most certainly do. Now, please try to concentrate. What are the three most important things that you need to know?" he asked before coming to a halt and folding his arms across his chest, much like her Spanish teacher, Señor Rena.

"Fine." Sophie gritted her teeth and read the answers off the sheet. "According to this, you can't eat and fly at the same time because bugs will get in your teeth."

"That's right." Malik proudly nodded in agreement. "Very important. Especially if you're ever visiting Australia. They have bugs the size of dinner plates, and if one of those gets stuck in your teeth, you're going to need a crowbar to get it out. And point two?"

"Don't talk on your cell phone while you're flying—well, we don't have a problem with that," Sophie said in a dark voice, since she was the only person in the world without a cell phone of her own. "And point three is, Never brake for pigeons because they are stupid and dumb and therefore don't matter. *What?*" Sophie stared at the piece of paper for a moment before screwing it up and throwing it at him. "Malik, you just made these up, didn't you?"

"That doesn't make them any less relevant," he insisted as he floated over to her desk and pulled a bag of M&M's out of the drawer. Sophie had no idea where they had come from, but she was gradually learning that sometimes it was better not to ask.

"Okay, fine. So now that we've done the theory, can I please start flying?" she begged as she walked over to the gorgeous new carpet, which was rolled up in the corner of the room. She had tried to unroll it when she'd first walked into her room, but Malik had stopped her and insisted on giving her rule after rule that she needed to know.

"Whoa there, missy. Not so fast." He suddenly appeared in front of her, chocolate flying out of his lips.

"Sophie, I don't think you understand how important carpet safety is. There are too many young, stupid djinns flying around these days, thinking that they're indestructible, and I have no intention of letting you become one of them."

"But if they're immortal, that sort of means that they *are* indestructible," Sophie reminded him as she reluctantly went over to her bed and sat down again.

"Do you think that this is a joke? That flying is funny?" He arched an eyebrow, and Sophie looked at him in surprise before shaking her head. He nodded in approval. "That's better. And now I think we can start looking at what your training will consist of. The first thing we need to do is get you to practice levitating. Once you have fully mastered that, then you can learn how to move the carpet through the sky. The final thing you'll need to master is the ability to teleport your carpet from one location to another. This will allow you to travel from your bedroom to Sheterum's mansion in a matter of seconds, without having your brain turned to mush. So... let's start with levitating. I want you to lift yourself off the ground. Can you do that?"

"Of course," she said as she swung her legs onto the bed and crossed them. Then she closed her eyes and visualized herself rising up off the comforter. A second later a familiar tingle went racing through her, and when she opened her eyes, she was floating a foot above her bed. She grinned at him as she held out her arms. "See? Easy.

Remember, we had to do transcendental conjuring before I went to see the djinn council."

"Parlor tricks." Malik gave a wave of his hand. "This is different because you need to keep your concentration no matter what." As he spoke he started to throw M&M's at her.

"Hey," Sophie lifted her hands to shield her face and immediately felt herself begin to wobble before she dropped down back onto the bed in a messy heap. She rubbed her legs and glared at Malik. "Why did you do that?"

"To show you how important it is to maintain your concentration. What would happen if I started throwing candy at you while you were flying?"

"I would think that you were having a fit since you never normally waste candy," Sophie quipped. She realized that he still wasn't laughing. Who knew that Malik would finally take something seriously? She let out a sigh. "Okay, I see your point. So I need to maintain my concentration at all times or else the carpet will fall."

"That is correct. And now that you can see my point, you will need to practice, practice, practice," he said in a solemn voice as he shoved a handful of M&M's into his mouth and made himself comfortable on the swivel chair next to her desk. "So let's try it again, and this time I want you to stay up. Are you ready?"

"Ready." Sophie nodded as she once again visualized herself lifting up off the ground. A second later Malik started to throw the candy, but this time she was prepared, and after five minutes of hovering in midair, Malik nodded his head in approval.

"Excellent," he said as he got to his feet and let three empty packets of M&M's drop to the bedroom floor. She was pretty sure that he hadn't thrown *that* much candy at her. "That was very well done. So now I want you to take this textbook and start reciting the flying code while you continue to levitate."

Sophie dropped back down to the bed and examined the large manual he was pointing to. The cover read *Flying Code*, and it looked like it weighed a hundred pounds. "You want me to learn this entire book while I'm floating up off the ground?" Sophie blinked. "That will take hours."

"Exactly," Malik agreed. "But you're such a quick learner that I'm sure you will have it all done by the time I get back, and then we can think about letting you touch the carpet."

"Really?" Sophie started to say before the rest of his words sunk in. "Hang on a minute, what do you mean 'when I come back'? Where are you going to be?"

"I promised Philippe I would play a round of golf with him," Malik said, as if it was the most obvious thing in the world. "Of course, his version of golf isn't exactly—"

"What?" Sophie yelped as she dropped the heavy leather-bound manual, which she had just picked up. "No. You can't just go off and play golf. You need to stay here and help me with my levitating. Malik, this is important. If I can't fly the carpet in time, then I won't be able to save my dad. You said yourself that Sheterum hardly ever leaves his mansion. This could be our only window of opportunity."

"I couldn't agree more, which is why you need to have complete silence so that you can concentrate. After all, you don't want to land on all of the eggs."

"What eggs?" Sophie said, while resisting the urge to throw something at her djinn guide. Instead, she had to content herself with gritting her teeth.

"Did I forget to mention the eggs?" Malik said as he floated over to his man bag and pulled out a carton of eggs, which he spread out across the bed below where Sophie had just been levitating.

"Yes, you forgot to mention the eggs," Sophie growled.

"Well, that was a close call," he said, smoothing down his shirt. "But thankfully, we caught it in time. *You're still looking annoyed.* Would it help if I told you that I was also going to search for Manny?"

"You are?"

"No." He gave an unrepentant smile. "But I'm happy to lie if that will make you feel better. So, here's the new plan. You stay here and levitate without smashing the eggs and learn the flying code by heart. Meanwhile, I'll go and play a nice, relaxing game of golf and put my yang back in line with my yin, *and search for Manny.* Then when I get back, we can start on the next stage. Yes?"

"No." She gave a firm shake of her head, but before she could stop him Malik snapped his fingers and disappeared from sight, leaving only a bag of Cheetos, numerous M&M's, and a dozen eggs behind. Sophie let out a groan and then reminded herself she was a positive person who would never want to harm her djinn guide. No matter how annoying he was. So instead she grabbed the heavy *Flying Code* and opened it to the first page. Then she visualized herself levitating and angled herself into position so that she was hovering a foot over the eggs on her bed. All she needed to do was think happy thoughts and remember that as long as she nailed her flying, in two weeks she would be seeing her dad again.

ON TUESDAY MORNING SOPHIE YAWNED AS SHE carefully put on her Eddie Henry guitar pick necklace and finished getting ready for school. She had spent most of the previous night levitating above her bed while softly reciting the *Flying Code*, which she had to say was full of the most stupid rules she had ever seen in her life.

After all, why would you have to give way to a djinn who was wearing a blue turban but not to a djinn who was wearing a red turban? It made no sense at all, and of course she couldn't ask Malik because he hadn't bothered to come back from his golfing trip. Not that she was worried about him, since once he had gone out for an ice cream and had come back three days later with a T-shirt that had been signed by the entire cast of *Cats*. From the West End in London. She just hoped that he wasn't being quite as adventurous this time around because she was desperate to keep going with her flying-carpet training.

Plus, there was still the small issue of how they were going to break into Sheterum's house. In fact, the more she thought about it, the more irresponsible she realized Malik was being by just disappearing. She was considering trying to summon him again when her mom called out to tell her that breakfast was ready.

Sophie flicked off the music she had been listening to and picked up the manual from where it was sitting on her bed. Then she tucked the art auction brochure inside the cover and took it over to her sock drawer, where the small vial of Solomon's Elixir was carefully hidden. She took the vial out for a moment and studied the shimmering amber liquid inside. Considering it was the most-sought-after elixir in the djinn world, it had been surprisingly easy to make. There was no chanting, meditating, or even leaving something during a lunar eclipse. Just lots of pounding, pasting, and waiding (which, she had discovered on the Internet, was a bit like stirring). But according to Malik, the secret was in the measuring, and that's what her father had obviously spent his life on perfecting.

It seemed impossible that something so insignificant looking would actually free her father. But then again, since Sophie had accidently managed to get herself bound to Melissa Tait, she understood all too well how strange the whole system was. Still, hers was not to question why, and so she hid everything away, glad that her mom wasn't a serial snooper, before grabbing her backpack and hurrying downstairs to the kitchen.

Meg was already in there, sullenly staring at a plate of

pancakes, which were burned to within an inch of their life. Even Mr. Jaws was looking at them dubiously, but the minute Sophie walked in he turned his attention to her as he began to hiss. She ignored him and sat down.

"So what's the special occasion?" she asked; her mom tended to make breakfast only every now and then— and unfortunately, this appeared to be one of those "now" times. As she spoke she wished that her pancakes would taste better than they looked and did the same for Meg's—there was no mention of not being able to use her powers to save them from food poisoning. A familiar tingle went through her, and she took a cautious bite. They now tasted like waffles.

"No special occasion." Her mom gave a casual shrug. "It's just since I delivered my latest pottery order yesterday, I thought I'd cook breakfast. I didn't want you girls to think I'd been neglecting you."

"I don't mind being neglected," Meg immediately retorted, still refusing to touch the blackened pancakes, despite the fact that Sophie was giving her an encouraging nod. "Especially when it means I can go and eat breakfast at Jessica's house. *And what's wrong with your hair? It looks weird.*"

"There's nothing wrong with my hair." Her mom automatically reached up and touched her shoulder-length blonde hair, which was once again neatly brushed and falling around her face in a shiny curtain. "I'm not in my studio today, so I thought I would make an effort."

"Well, I think you look very nice," Sophie said in a positive voice, since, when their dad had first left them, her mom had sometimes gone for weeks without even looking at a hairbrush. Maybe the fact that she was doing so now meant that, on some level, she knew that he would be home soon? The thought made Sophie smile, and she shoveled another piece of burned pancake into her mouth.

"I don't like it," Meg suddenly announced. "I think you look better when your hair's all messy. And I don't like these pancakes either." Then without another word she pushed her plate away, flounced into the living room, and turned on the television. A second later the sound of a shark documentary blared out at them. Sophie looked at her mom in surprise.

"What's wrong with her? Has she had another fight with Jessica?" Sophie asked. Her sister regularly switched between loving and hating her best friend, Jessica Dalton, depending on what day of the week it was.

"I don't think so." Her mom shook her neatly brushed hair and started to gather up Meg's untouched breakfast. "She's been in a funny mood for the last few days. I was hoping she might've mentioned something to you?"

"No, sorry." Sophie finished off her burned-pancakes-that-tasted-like-waffles and then felt a little guilty as she realized how distracted she had been with making Solomon's Elixir and practicing her flying lessons, not to mention spending so much time with Jonathan. But before she could answer, Kara and Harvey poked their heads through the back door. Harvey took one look at the burned pancakes and widened his eyes in horror. Sophie giggled as she jumped to her feet and grabbed her backpack. "Anyway, I'd better go."

"Okay, well, have a great day." Her mom planted a kiss on her cheek before turning toward the living room, no doubt to start trying to convince Meg to get ready for school. The minute they were outside her two friends turned to her.

"So did you go flying? How was it?" Harvey demanded.

"Were you careful?" Kara asked in concern. "You didn't let Malik talk you into doing anything stupid, did you? No loop-the-looping, I hope."

"Definitely no loop-the-looping." Sophie shook her head. "Can you believe that for once in his life, Malik was incredibly serious? He won't even let me near the carpet until I've perfected my levitating and memorized the *Flying Code*. Though he did say that if he was satisfied that I knew everything, then he would let me have a go this afternoon, as long as he could get some kind of stabilizer for it, which I think is flying-carpet talk for training wheels."

"Jeez, sounds like he's turned into the DMV." Harvey rolled his eyes in an unexpected fit of disgust. "Why can't he just let you fly it already?"

"Harvey, you were the one who didn't even want me to get a skateboard because you saw a movie about a ten-year-old girl who fell on her head," Sophie reminded him as the bus pulled up in front of the school and they all got out.

"Yes, but that was a skateboard. They are highly dangerous. Whereas this is completely different." Harvey gave a dismissive wave of his hands, and his normally concerned expression was replaced by one of eleven-year-old-boy excitement. "I mean, straight up, there's nothing cooler than this."

"Well, hopefully Malik will let me get on the carpet soon. I spent most of the night levitating, and when I woke up this morning, I discovered that my hairbrush was up by the ceiling. It was like I was on the space shuttle. I guess I must've made it levitate in my sleep."

"That's crazy," Kara started to say, but before she could finish, her cell phone started to beep. She looked up and grinned. "It's from Patrick." However, her smile faded as she studied the screen.

"What is it?" Sophie asked in alarm. "Has something happened?"

"Yes. I mean, no. Well, I'm not sure." Kara shook her head as if trying to collect her thoughts, and she gripped her cell phone tightly. "Patrick's in the auditorium, and it looks like someone has vandalized Colin's tail. Anyway, he said that it's not bad but that he wanted me to know."

"Kara, that's awful." Sophie's voice shook with sympathy. While she didn't exactly understand the whole papier-mâché process, she *did* know how important it was to her friend. "Can he be fixed?"

"Patrick thinks so," Kara conceded as she hitched her

bag farther over her shoulder. "Would you guys mind if I bailed? I want to have a look at him before homeroom."

"Of course not." Harvey quickly shook his head. "I'll walk with you as far as the computer labs."

"Thanks," Kara said, a frown still plastered to her face. "Who would want to hurt a poor innocent flying monkey?"

"I've got no idea." Sophie gave her friend a quick hug. "But hopefully we can find out soon. I'll see you guys in homeroom."

"Thanks." Kara sniffed as she and Harvey hurried down the hallway as fast as their long legs would take them. Once her friends were gone, Sophie headed for her locker (which, in geographical terms, was in Siberia).

Out of habit, she glanced over to Jonathan's locker, before remembering that he was going to be away all day at a basketball tournament. Stupid basketball. Still, even looking at the spot where he stood every day made her smile as she busied herself sorting out her books. But it wasn't until she had shut her locker that she realized that something like snow was landing on her head.

She craned her neck toward the ceiling and let out a groan when she caught sight of Malik, sitting cross-legged on top of her locker and eating a croissant. She quickly brushed the crumbs out of her hair and tried to figure out why he was wearing a black beret and a blue-and-white-striped T-shirt and had a thin black mustache penciled in on his upper lip.

"Too much?" he immediately asked as he touched the mustache. Sophie ignored the question as she glared up at him.

"Seriously, where have you been?" she hissed in a low voice, since she had long discovered that talking to a ghost in public places tended to make her look like a crazy person, and right now crazy wasn't a look she was going for.

"I've been playing golf," he said, floating down to the floor. Then he wrinkled his nose. "I thought I told you that."

"Yes, but you've been gone since yesterday afternoon. How long does a golf game take?" Sophie demanded and nodded her head in the direction of the janitor's closet just beside her locker. It had kind of become their impromptu office—not only was it private, but they had never yet seen a janitor in it.

"Not very long," he explained as he followed her in. "Only problem was that Philippe had a hankering to go to this course in Bordeaux. And trust me, he is one dead djinn who does not like taking no for an answer. Still, it wasn't all bad. We did have some nice snails."

Sophie blinked. "You went to France?"

"Well, yes, why else would I be wearing this ridiculous outfit?" Malik asked, looking confused. "You know, I don't mean to criticize, but for a positive person, you're sounding a bit stressed. So what's the emergency?"

"Remember my dad? How we need to rescue him?"

Sophie asked in a tight voice. "I was practicing my levitation all night and learning those stupid flying rules while you were playing golf."

"Hey, playing golf is very therapeutic. You should try it sometime. And speaking of therapeutic, I don't suppose you could rustle me up some Cheetos?"

For a moment Sophie was tempted to say no, but then she reminded herself that, despite all of his faults, there was no way she could've managed any of this on her own. Plus, Malik was under the mistaken impression that his pouting made her feel sorry for him. When actually all it did was remind her that everyone over the age of fifteen was insane.

She closed her eyes and wished for some Cheetos, and then, as a joke, instead of making them appear in Malik's outstretched hand, she used her transcendental conjuring skills to make the bag levitate next to his head.

"Ha-ha, very funny," he retorted as he tried to grab them three times before Sophie finally stopped.

"Just trying to show you how much work I did last night." Sophie grinned before shooting him a hopeful look. "So I don't suppose you got any news about where this mysterious Manny is when you were playing golf?"

"Sorry, not yet," Malik said between mouthfuls of Cheetos. "But my buddy Eric did leave me a message on Twitter to say that he might've spotted him. Of course, Eric once thought he saw Godzilla before discovering it was actually just a mouse in some good lighting."

"You fill me with confidence," Sophie said as she hitched her backpack over her shoulder. "Anyway, I'd better go to my homeroom, but Malik, if you hear anything, please let me know *immediately.*"

"Of course I will." Malik looked offended, as if he had never forgotten to tell her something before. Sophie ignored him as she opened the door of the janitor's closet. She was just about to step out when she saw Melissa Tait leaning against Sophie's locker, stroking her perfect blonde hair in an ominous fashion. Great, that was all she needed.

6

$S$OPHIE STEPPED BACK INTO THE CLOSET AND LET out a long groan. Melissa Tait was waiting for her out in the hallway, which, in Sophie's experience, was *never* a good thing. Especially considering that her little effort to help Melissa yesterday had apparently been a major fail. She turned to where Malik was busily upending the Cheetos bag to get the last of the cheesy goodness into his mouth.

"Okay," she gulped. "We've got a problem. Melissa Tait is standing in front of my locker, and while the positive thinker in me would like to think it was just some weird coincidence, I'm pretty sure it's not."

"She is?" Malik asked with interest as he poked his head through the closed door, leaving only his body inside the closet. "Wow, you're right. That is a problem," he called out from the other side of the door in a disembodied voice. "She looks mad. Is this because of the whole 'you made her boyfriend dump her' thing?"

Sophie sighed and shook her head. "Actually, I think

it's more of the 'I tried to help her with her history assignment by conjuring up some extra books for her in the library' thing. I only did it to make her stop texting Jonathan so he could ask me to his parents' anniversary party. Unfortunately, I don't think the books were there, so now she's annoyed with me."

*"Again?"* Malik added as he pulled his head back into the closet and rolled his eyes. "You really do have a habit of annoying her."

"I know. It's uncanny, and since I've already tried the 'let's be friends' approach, which didn't work, I think I'm going to have to completely avoid her. Unfortunately, I have no idea how. I mean, from the looks of it, she's going to stay at my locker until the bell rings. What am I going to do?"

"Well, personally, I would take that as an excuse to sit in here and watch *High School Musical* on an iPad, *but*," he quickly added as he paused in the midst of pulling an iPad out of the ugly man bag that was slung over his shoulder, as if catching Sophie's annoyed glare. "In your case, let's look at your options. You could always blow up your locker. That would make her move."

"Malik," Sophie growled.

"Okay, so no blowing up lockers. Let's think. You could do a memory wipe on her so that she won't be able to remember the most recent annoying thing you did. That's fun. Oh, or my personal favorite, you could create a mini-tornado that—"

"Do you have any suggestions that don't involve blowing up the school or messing with her mind? I mean, all I want to do is get past her."

"Well," he said in a disappointed voice, "I suppose you could just use your invisibility patch. I mean, it's not really what I would call a classic, but then again, you're probably not classic material. I, on the other hand, am pure classic. I remember this one time when I needed to create a diversion, and it was so successful that they still talk about it today. In fact, I don't like to boast, but they called it 'the Malik' and—"

"Wait. Back up," Sophie cut him off and wrinkled her nose. "What are you talking about? What's an invisibility patch?"

"Oh, did I forget to mention them? I got you some yesterday when I was playing golf—because that's just the kind of considerate, generous djinn guide that I am," he said as he pulled a piece of paper out of his man bag.

"But what is it for? Why do I need an invisibility patch?" Sophie asked. Instinct told her that it would probably make her invisible, but experience had taught her that trusting her instincts when Malik was involved wasn't always a good thing.

"For your flying lessons, of course. You don't think I'm going to let you fly around in your backyard so that people can actually see you? In case you haven't noticed, humans don't like anything out of the ordinary. Especially when it comes to ugly flying carpets."

Sophie chose to ignore his comments about her beautiful carpet. "So how do invisibility patches work?" she asked.

"Simple. You just put one on your arm and activate the magic, and next thing you know, you're invisible. See," he added before disappearing from sight, as if trying to prove his point. Then he reappeared and took a bow. "So what do you think? Do you want to use a patch to sneak past Melissa?"

"Of course I do," Sophie agreed, narrowing her eyes. "But Malik, before I put one on, you need to think very, very hard. Is there *anything* about these patches that you're forgetting to tell me? Like that if I use one I will suddenly grow a tail. Or turn pink. Or turn pink and *taily.*"

"You wound me with your words." Malik pressed his hand to his chest as if he had been mortally injured. However, when he realized that Sophie didn't seem to care about his fake injury, he just shrugged. "No. There are definitely no side effects. Unless you count the awesomeness of being invisible. Eventually, of course, you'll be able to turn invisible on your own, but right now, for a noob like yourself, a patch is the best way. Plus, since you're going to need them when we start the next stage of your flying practice this afternoon, you might as well get used to them."

"Okay, I'm in. How long will it take for it to work?"

"About one second," Malik said; he peeled a black dot

off the page and pressed it to her skin. A second later it brightened in color before disappearing entirely. "There, now that it's embedded, all you need to do is click your fingers and say 'invisible.'"

"And?" Sophie prompted, but Malik just looked at her blankly.

"And nothing."

"Yeah, right. As if it will work just because I click my fingers and say 'invisible,'" Sophie said, doing just that. "Because—" But the rest of her words died on her lips as a small ripple flashed through her body, leaving a weird twittery feeling in her fingers.

She hurried over to the small chipped mirror hanging up in the closet. No reflection stared back at her, though when she glanced down at herself, she could still see her body clearly. Sophie rubbed her eyes and stared into the mirror again. Nothing. She still couldn't see her reflection. She lifted up a finger and poked herself in the face. Ouch. She could feel it but not see it. Malik, who was looking at her with interest, and could obviously see her despite the magic, just gave a casual wave of his arm.

"You were saying something?" he inquired in a polite voice that was at odds with the slightly smug expression on his Zac-like face. Sophie widened her eyes.

"How come I can still see my body, but when I look in the mirror, there is nothing there?"

"How should I know? I'm not an alchemist who deals

with matters of science and magic. All I know is that you need to trust the mirror. If it says you're invisible, then you're invisible. So? What do you think?"

"I think it's amazing," she said, while privately congratulating herself on spending half of fourth grade practicing how to snap her fingers. She knew it would come in handy someday. She finally dragged her gaze away from her invisible reflection and turned back to Malik. "Okay, so what else do I need to know?"

"Two things. First is that while no one can see you, they can definitely hear you, so no heavy breathing or talking. Well, not unless you want to freak them out— and trust me, nothing is more embarrassing than thinking that you're invisible when you're sniffing someone's hair and then you discover that they can hear you panting."

Sophie stared at him for a moment before deciding that there was no answer to that statement. "And the second thing?"

"The second thing is that when you want to turn back to normal, you just click your fingers and say 'visible.'"

"Right." Sophie nodded as she ticked off her fingers. "I can remember that." Then she checked her reflection in the mirror one more time (phew, still invisible) and slowly opened the closet door so that she could peer out into the hallway.

Melissa was looking even more annoyed than ever as she leaned against Sophie's locker, while her Tait-bots hovered just to the left of her. If this didn't work, Sophie was going to be in big trouble, and for a moment she considered just staying in the janitor's closet until after class had started. The only thing stopping her was the fact that her mom would freak if she got into any more trouble at school.

"Hello, someone could grow old and die in here," Malik said with a cough from behind her, obviously a lot more used to being invisible than Sophie was. She took one final deep breath and stepped out into the hallway. The moment she did so, Terry Richards, a sixth-grade band guy, almost knocked her out with his oboe case. Sophie only just managed to scramble out of the way in time, and she put her hand over her mouth to stop herself from squealing out in protest. Once she regained her composure, however, she realized that the reason he had almost knocked her out was because he couldn't see her.

Nice. Sophie tentatively walked toward her locker, her confidence growing as she stepped past the Tait-bots. None of them even blinked at her, which was a first. Finally, she reached her locker and stood in front of Melissa. Sophie paused for a moment and waved her hand up and down in front of Melissa's perfect (but sour-looking) face. But instead of even noticing, Melissa merely turned to her Tait-bots and snapped her fingers.

"You know, nothing annoys me more than having to wait for idiots who don't even have the decency to show up." The seventh grader pouted as she and her friends swayed off in the other direction. The minute they were gone, Malik turned up beside her.

"Seriously, did you *see* that?" Sophie demanded as she waved her arms in front of a group of kids who were walking past her. None of them even noticed her. "It worked."

"Well, yeah. I mean, otherwise you'd just be the girl who was walking around putting your hand in everyone's face," Malik said as the bell rang. Sophie reluctantly stopped her arm waving.

"Sorry, but you've got to admit that it's pretty cool." She grinned.

"You don't have to tell me," Malik assured her as he walked over to a sixth grader and plucked one of the M&M's out of his packet and grinned.

"So what now?" Sophie asked, trying to ignore Malik's blatant theft as she caught sight of Harvey and Kara walking toward them. "Are you going to stay at school today?"

"Are you kidding me?" He shuddered. "I mean, it was fun watching you mess with Melissa Tait, but I would rather have my eyeballs pulled out and pickled than have to sit through any more of your classes. Especially since most of your teachers seem like complete imbeciles. Anyway, I thought I'd go and catch up on a spot of shopping."

"Er, okay," Sophie started to say, but before she could finish, Malik disappeared in a puff of Cheetos crumbs just as Kara and Harvey came to a halt next to where Sophie was standing.

Kara wrinkled her nose as she looked right through

her. "Okay, that was weird. One minute Malik was here, and then he just disappeared."

"I know. And where's Sophie? Why would Malik be at her locker when she's not around? It's not even like it's lasagna day in the cafeteria," Harvey added, just as Sophie said, "Visible," and snapped her fingers.

She then watched her friends yelp in surprise.

Kara's face drained of color, and she tentatively reached out and poked Sophie's arm to check that it was real. Next to her Harvey just stared.

"Okay, what just happened?" Kara croaked. "Where did you come from?"

"It's a long story." Sophie linked arms with her two friends and told them about everything that had happened. Then she grinned. Let the fun and games commence.

7

AND YOU'RE SURE THAT THERE ARE NO SIDE EF-
fects?" Harvey asked for the zillionth time that afternoon as they waited at the bus stop.

"Harvey, we've been over this," Kara said in her calm-
est voice as she hastily sketched a soothing picture of a
tropical beach and thrust it into his hands to try to help
him relax. "Malik has promised that it's completely safe."

"Yes, but since when do we believe everything that
Malik says?" Harvey pointed out.

"Well, this time I think we can trust him. Did you not
see me turn invisible?" Sophie chimed in, still completely buzzing from her newly found talent. It had taken her
most of homeroom and half of first period to convince her
friends that she could really turn invisible, and even then
it was only when she started talking to them while they
couldn't see her that they finally believed her. The best
part had been sneaking up behind Señor Rena and moving his Spanish dictionary around on the desk as everyone was leaving the classroom. Not to mention the fact

that she had successfully avoided Melissa Tait for the rest of the day. Result.

"And don't forget the most important thing: now that Sophie has the patch, she can move on to the next stage of her flying lessons," Kara reminded Harvey, and he grudgingly nodded his head in agreement.

"Good point. So do you think he'll let you get onto the carpet today?"

"I hope so." Sophie crossed her fingers and resisted the urge to make herself invisible again (not because she needed to hide from anyone, but just because she could).

"By the way, I talked to my mom, and she said that we can go to the mall tomorrow afternoon. Is that okay?" Kara asked. "I mean, I understand if you need to do more flying practice."

"Of course I'm coming," Sophie said. "I wouldn't miss it for anything. We need to find you the perfect outfit for Saturday. Plus, I still need shoes, and I can't conjure anything up if I haven't seen the ones I want yet."

They spent the rest of the bus trip home helping Kara decide which bracelets she should wear. Well, Sophie and Kara decided; Harvey just sat next to them rolling his eyes. But as the bus got closer to her house, all Sophie could think about was that soon she would be learning to fly.

"Okay, so what happens if it starts to rain? Do you, (a) do a weather spell, (b) conjure up a raincoat, or (c) increase your speed to try to beat the shower?" Malik quizzed as he marched along the grass, a surprisingly stern expression on his face. It got sterner as he looked down to where Sophie was sitting on her invisible carpet, with her invisible legs crossed, trying to hide her not-so-invisible boredom.

When they had first come outside, it had felt strange to roll out the carpet on the grass and sit there, knowing that, despite the fact her mom was in the kitchen and Meg and Jessica were having a rowdy game of shark next door, none of them could see her. Of course, then Malik had pounded her brain with question after question and the awkwardness had quickly given away to annoyance.

"The answer is 'b.'" She forced herself not to scream as she gave him a pleading glance. "Now please, you've asked me every question in the *Flying Code* at least three times. At this rate we will never be ready in time to get my dad."

"Fine." Malik relented as he reached out and grabbed the second finger of the Twix bar that Sophie had conjured up for him. "So if you're ready, I think it's time for you to try to fly up to the roof of the house. And don't worry, because the stabilizers are attached, so you can't accidently get caught in any wind currents. But I mean it, if you even think about doing anything that I don't like, then it will be back to levitating in your bedroom. Are we clear?"

"Clear." She nodded in agreement as he instructed her

to empty her mind the way he had taught her so that she was focused. According to Malik, she needed to use her body like a steering wheel so if she wanted to go up, she had to tilt her head skyward—gently, he had added after the rug had tried to go vertical. It was the same for turning left, turning right, or lowering herself back down to the ground. Then once she mastered the basics of flying, he would teach her how to teleport so that they could get to their destination a lot faster. Apparently, this involved a lot of blinking—

"Hello, I might be a dead djinn, but I can assure you that I'm not getting any younger. Could you move it along, please?" Malik cut through her thoughts, and Sophie let out a groan as she began to concentrate. First she had to make sure she wasn't clutching the carpet too tightly, because doing so apparently affected the aerodynamic qualities or something. Then she carefully angled her head so that it was pointing toward the sky. For a moment nothing happened, and Sophie caught her breath. Before she could ask Malik what had gone wrong, though, the carpet gave a little shake and then gently started to float up into the air until she was level with the kitchen window.

"Nice," Malik said, and Sophie realized that he was now sitting next to her on the carpet. She grinned and tilted her head to the right. The rug responded, and this time she only just resisted the urge to squeal in excitement as it floated past the living room window. "Now, you just need to use your hands to keep a gentle pressure on the rug. That will keep it going at a level speed. *Well, go on then.*"

"Really? I can fly past the house? Are you sure that I'm ready?"

"I'm sure." He nodded his head. "You've got the stabilizers on, and if anything goes wrong, they'll switch to automatic control. Unless, of course, you decide to fly into the direct path of a kite; if you do that, you will be untangling yourself for a week."

"Right, avoid all kites." Sophie made a mental note as she felt the woolen fibers of the carpet push into her palms. She increased the pressure, and the carpet gained in speed; soon her house was behind her.

She lifted her head to move farther up into the air, away from the hazards of chimneys and power lines.

The wind brushed Sophie's face, and she could feel her fine hair blowing out behind her. Below, tiny cars were zooming past, looking like they were from a Matchbox set. It was breathtaking, and part of her longed to reach her arms out wide, *Titanic*-style. Then she remembered that her hands were helping her to keep the carpet going, so she sensibly kept them where they were.

"Okay." Malik's voice was suddenly in her ear. "Let's try some close-quarters flying. To do that, you need to reduce your speed and get nearer to the ground. This is particularly handy if you're chasing an ifrit who thinks that running away from a poker debt is a good idea."

For a moment Sophie blinked, then gently lifted her hands off the carpet. She felt it slow down beneath them. Then she leaned forward, and the carpet gently headed back toward the ground below.

"Excellent." Malik nodded in approval. "Now increase your speed just enough so that you don't crash." Sophie obediently did what he said, and soon they were flying just above a tree-lined street. Malik pointed to a small park at the end of the street. "Now, let's see how well you can land this thing. The trick is to make sure that you don't stall just before you come to a stop, or you'll fall off and do a face plant."

Sophie bit down on her lip as she straightened her spine and felt the carpet respond to the command. Then she lifted her hands slowly up off the woolen pile, and the carpet slid to a smooth halt.

She had done it!

She, Sophie Campbell, had flown a carpet! She let out an exhilarating scream, and this time she did raise her hands into the air in victory. Unfortunately, the carpet hadn't quite touched the ground, and, as Malik had predicted, she went face-first into the grass. Still, even as she untangled herself and looked over to where Malik was rolling his eyes, she still couldn't stop smiling. That was possibly the best thing she had ever done in her life.

Sophie jumped to her feet, adrenaline still buzzing through her veins. She shot Malik an excited look. "Okay, so what now? Can you teach me some tricks? Oh, what about standing up? That would be great. Or maybe we could—"

"Get an ice cream," Malik interrupted. "The first rule of all flying lessons is that you need to take an ice-cream break." As he spoke he nodded over to a fancy-looking ice-cream store at the far end of the park.

"Did you direct us here on purpose?"

"Of course," Malik said. "I felt like ice cream, and what's the point of your practicing your landing where there's no ice-cream store? That doesn't make any sense."

"Yes, but—" Sophie started to say, before catching sight of a shoe store right next to the ice-cream store. Then she put her hand over her mouth so Malik wouldn't see her smiling; but seriously, it was like the Universe was commanding her to go and look in there. She could definitely get used to this.

TEN MINUTES AND TWO CARTONS OF FULL-FAT
cookies-and-cream ice cream later, Sophie and Malik
were once again up in the air and on their way home.
There also might have been the most adorable pair of
nude-colored, peep-toe boots sitting in her lap. Not that
she'd stolen them from the store; she had simply seen
them in the window and wished for her own pair. And
they were perfect. She had been wanting something with
a heel to make her look taller, but since she couldn't actually walk in heels, not to mention the fact that her mom
would flip out, she had compromised on a small wedge,
which gave her an extra inch without increasing her
chances of her breaking her neck.

For a moment she felt bad that she hadn't chosen them
with Kara, but then she realized it would simply give
them more time to shop for Kara's own outfit and really
that's what was—

"Hey, hello there. Anyone at home? Because if you
don't turn now, you'll probably hit that bird, and then

you'll be picking feathers out of your hair for a week. Of course, that is a valid lifestyle choice, and if it's something that you really want to do, then be my guest," Malik said. It sounded like he was still a bit put out that she hadn't followed his advice and conjured up the hot pink clogs that he'd taken a liking to.

"Sorry." Sophie quickly steered the carpet to the left of the bird, and a couple of minutes later she caught sight of her house not far below. She sucked in a breath of air and focused her thoughts, determined that this landing would be smoother than the last.

"That's it." Malik nodded his approval before leaning back, obviously unable to stop pretending that he was the one flying the carpet. "Now, you want to slow down your speed as much as you can. And then I want you to think about the basement."

"What?" Sophie turned to him in surprise, causing the carpet to wobble. She quickly refocused until it was once again still. Then she took a deep breath and resisted the urge to wipe away the sweat that was beading up on her brow. "So tell me why I am thinking about the basement? I hate the basement. More importantly, I hate the spiders in the basement."

"I am not a fan of it, either, but since the carpet is too big to land in your room, it's the only place for you to practice teleporting. Besides, it's not like the spiders in your basement are going to eat you. I mean, their teeth aren't even big enough to pierce the skin. Of course, if it was a Tibetan blue-lipped spider that would be a different story altogether, because those bad boys have fangs like you wouldn't believe. But those little guys in your basement are completely harmless."

"You fill me with confidence," Sophie said in a dry voice, as she tried not to think about giant fanged spiders and focused on her flying. "So you're saying that I just need to think of the basement and that's where I'll land?"

"That's right," Malik said. "Oh, but don't forget to visualize a large bubble around the carpet before you do that. It will stop your face from feeling like it's been pounded by gale-force winds. Then you just need to blink three times."

Sophie looked at him to see if he was joking, but it was impossible to tell. So she took a deep breath and prayed that the Universe knew what it was doing. Then she focused on the basement and pictured a giant bubble surrounding the carpet. Once that was done, Sophie blinked three times before she felt a gentle tugging sensation in her stomach.

"Nice work," Malik said as Sophie cautiously opened her eyes. She let out a small whoop of excitement as she realized they were in the basement. She quickly uncrossed her legs and shook her limbs to get her circulation going again as she stared around her. Then she clicked her fingers and said, "Visible," before checking herself in the chipped mirror that was hanging up near an old workbench. Apart from the fact that her blonde hair now resembled a bird's nest, she looked the same as she always did. She turned back to Malik and grinned.

"I did it! We flew, we teleported, and we shopped. That's amazing."

"No," Malik said in confusion. "Amazing is the way Jell-O dissolves in your mouth when you eat it. Flying a carpet and teleporting and conjuring up items is just magic."

"Er, right," Sophie said as adrenaline continued to course through her veins. She tried to ignore it as she took her new shoes off the carpet and quickly rolled it up before wishing it would go into the far corner of the basement. A second later it did, and she turned back to Malik. "But that was seriously amazing. Thank you."

"You're welcome," Malik said as he floated over to the collection of packing boxes that held all of her dad's old possessions. When they had been gathering up the ingredients for Solomon's Elixir, they had checked the boxes and been delighted to discover that some of the ingredients were neatly packed down at the bottom of one in between some old shoes. "Besides, you did exceptionally well for your first time, and if you keep this up, then you'll definitely be ready to fly to Los Angeles."

"Really?" Happiness radiated off her, and for a moment Sophie closed her eyes and pictured what it would be like to see her father again for the first time in four years. Would he think she had grown? That she totally rocked a flying carpet? That she—

"Well, would you look at that?" Malik's voice broke her thoughts, and she opened her eyes to see that he was holding her father's favorite David Bowie T-shirt up to his chest to see if it would fit. "Tariq the Awesome and I are the same size. I wonder if he would mind if I borrowed this?"

"I mind." Sophie immediately pulled it away from him and clutched it to her chest. "Besides, my dad will be home soon, and then he'll need all of his old clothes," she added in a firm voice.

"Or alternatively, he might decide that it's time to say good-bye to the old part of his life and get ready for a new chapter. In which case, he wouldn't even miss one little impossible-to-buy-anymore David Bowie *Serious Moonlight* concert T-shirt… *Okay, fine, so the T-shirt stays.*"

"Thank you," Sophie said, feeling bad that she was keeping it from him after all his help. She wasn't even sure if she could explain her reasons. "It's just, the thing is, I—"

But the rest of her words were cut off when the basement door opened and her mom walked down the stairs, looking very confused.

"Sophie, what on earth are you doing down here? I've been looking for you everywhere. Didn't you hear me calling you?"

"O-oh," Sophie stammered, since she had completely forgotten that there was a definite drawback to practicing invisible flying when her mom was at home. "Well, here I am."

"Yes, but I'm still not sure why you're down here. And who were you talking to?"

"See, it's like she can just feel my presence," Malik said as he puffed his chest forward and gave a coy little half wave. Despite the fact that Sophie's mom couldn't see him, Malik was convinced that they had a connection because they were friends on Facebook. Sophie was convinced he was delusional. "Oh, and I like what she's done to her hair. It's cute."

"Of course no one's here with me," Sophie said in a firm voice as she shot Malik a warning look.

"Really?" Her mom looked around in confusion. "Because I was sure I heard you talking to someone."

Again Malik grinned, but Sophie ignored him as she searched her mind for a suitable excuse. She could hardly say that she had been practicing her carpet-flying skills, and since she didn't own a cell phone she couldn't say she had been talking on it, which meant there was only one thing to do.

"I was...er...talking to a spider," Sophie finally said, resisting the urge to shudder.

"A spider?" Her mom raised an eyebrow in surprise. "But you hate spiders."

"Yes, yes, I do," Sophie reluctantly agreed. "But since I'm such a positive person, who prefers to be at one with the Universe, I'm trying to make myself get to know them. I mean, maybe I've been misjudging them all these years? Anyway, I think the spider and I have come to an understanding now."

"You know, you really are the worst liar I've ever heard. You could've just said that you were singing a Neanderthal Joe song," Malik said in a helpful voice that only she could hear. The fact that he had a good point didn't improve her mood. "Anyway, as delightful as it is to watch you talk about spiders, I've got to go." Without another word he snapped his fingers and disappeared from sight.

"Well, I'm happy that you and the spider have cleared the air," her mom said before catching sight of the David Bowie T-shirt, which was still in Sophie's hand. Her mom's eyes filled with concern. "When I agreed not to throw away your father's things, I didn't think it would encourage you to spend so much time moping down here. Should I be worried?"

"Of course not," Sophie quickly responded. When her djinn powers had first come through, Sophie hadn't quite managed to make the most stellar start to sixth grade. That was one of the reasons why her mom had wanted to sell the house so that they could move to Montana. Not something that Sophie wanted to experience for a second time.

"Really? Because I'm not convinced, so how about you tell me the real reason? And this time I don't want to hear about any spiders."

Sophie chewed her lip for a moment and took a deep

breath. "I'm, er, saying good-bye to an old part of my life and getting ready for a new chapter," she improvised, using Malik's words. Besides, it wasn't really a lie; as soon as her dad was back it *would* be a whole new chapter. More importantly, it was obviously exactly what her mom wanted to hear, because the worry lines around her eyes instantly disappeared as Sophie put the T-shirt down.

"Oh, Sophie, I'm so pleased. And I know it's been a tough few years, but I really feel like things are starting to get better."

"Absolutely." Sophie nodded in agreement. "S-so... did you want to ask me something?"

"Oh, right. Yes, I did. Max Rivers just called. He's got Ryan staying with him for the week, and he wanted to know if you could babysit for him after school tomorrow for a couple of hours."

"What?" Sophie was immediately taken aback because not only was the six-year-old Ryan a biter of legendary status, but the last time Sophie had been at Mr. Rivers's house, she had managed to get herself turned into a djinn. And while logically she knew it was unlikely that he would accidently have another djinn-infested vase lying around, Sophie wasn't exactly eager to repeat the experience. She instantly shook her head. "I promised Kara I'd go with her and her mom to the mall. Not to mention all my homework." *Or the fact that she would rather stab herself in the leg with her scissors than have to be in the same room as Ryan the biter.*

"Well, you can do your homework at Max's house, and I'm sure that Kara would understand if you missed out on tomorrow's shopping trip. The thing is, I'd really appreciate it. Max has been such a wonderful help to me lately. He's the one who convinced Monica Tait to order so much of my work." Then her mom coughed. "Is there... a particular reason why you don't want to do it? Is there something you don't like about him?"

"What?" Sophie asked in surprise before quickly shaking her head. "No, I guess he's nice enough." Which was kind of true, since while she didn't like the fact that he had a crazy nephew and had managed to have a djinn-bound bottle in his basement, he seemed okay. Plus, there was the added advantage that he lived next door to Jonathan Tait, which was why Sophie had agreed to babysit Ryan the first time around. "The thing is, I really did promise Kara that—"

"Are those shoes I can see over there?" Her mom suddenly looked over Sophie's shoulder in the general direction of where the pair of nude-colored, peep-toe wedge boots were sitting. Sophie silently groaned as she realized too late that they weren't invisible. Thankfully, the basement lighting wasn't the best, and so Sophie quickly tried to block her mom's view while glancing in the other direction.

"S-shoes," she stammered. "I can't see any shoes."

"No, not that way," her mom said. "Over there. In the corner. I'm sure it's some—"

"So about this babysitting tomorrow. I'd love to do it," Sophie quickly broke in, and the moment her mom stopped looking in the direction of the shoes, Sophie made a quick wish, sending them to the back of her closet, while making a mental note never to shop and fly at the same time.

"Oh?" Her mom was immediately distracted as she looked at Sophie in delight. "You would? Sophie, that's wonderful. Max will be so thrilled."

"That makes two of us," Sophie lied as she followed her mom up the stairs and wiped her brow. That was way too close for comfort. Still, the important thing was that, according to Malik, with some more practice her flying skills would be good enough to rescue her dad. Suddenly, the idea of having to babysit Ryan the biter didn't seem so bad.

9

"SO, WHAT HAPPENED? I WANT TO KNOW EVERYTHING,"
Harvey demanded the next morning as they pushed
their way down the aisle of the bus and squeezed onto the
two-person bench seat, as was their habit.

"It was fantastic." Sophie grinned before proceeding to
tell them everything that had happened. Right down to
the ice cream and the shoes.

"Shoes?" Harvey shook his head in disgust, his long
bangs swinging. "You ruined a perfectly good flying ad-
venture by stopping to buy shoes?"

"Well, it was Malik's fault for wanting ice cream," Sophie protested, before remembering just what a nuisance
the shoes had been. She turned to Kara and took a deep
breath. "But actually, there is something I need to tell
you. I kind of promised that I would babysit Ryan the
biter after school today," she said, bracing herself for their
reaction.

Yep. There it was.

"You what?" Kara and Harvey yelped in unison, their

faces matching masks of horror. Kara added, "Why didn't you tell us about this first?"

"Because I knew that you would both freak out and start making faces. See." Sophie pointed to them both as proof.

"Yes, well, we're making faces because it is a very bad idea," Kara retorted. "A very, very bad idea. After all, if Mr. Rivers can keep a djinn in his basement, then there's no saying what else could be in there."

"Plus, don't forget that he has very strange body language," Harvey added. "I still haven't figured out if he's a serial killer or has an eating disorder, but there's definitely something weird about him."

"Look, you guys, I don't want to do it, either. Especially since I'm supposed to be going shopping with Kara at the mall."

"So don't do it," Kara immediately replied. "Just tell your mom that you can't cancel because it's a fashion emergency. I mean, I could totally buy the wrong outfit if you're not there."

"Of course you won't," Sophie assured her, since her friend, who was tall and willowy, tended to look amazing in pretty much anything she put on. Paint-splattered clothes included.

"Yes, but that doesn't change the fact that Mr. Rivers is evil," Harvey pointed out. "So if you just mention it to your mom, I'm sure she'll change her mind. I mean, she's hardly going to make you babysit for someone evil."

"I know it's not ideal, but Mr. Rivers has been helping her out loads lately with her pottery business. Plus, he had no idea that Malik was trapped in a vase in his basement," Sophie protested as the bus pulled into Robert Robertson Middle School and they all scrambled out. "Besides, it actually helps me with the tricky problem of how to explain to my mom that I could afford my new outfit for the anniversary party when she knows that I only have three bucks in my bank account. The important thing to remember is that Malik said that flying was going really well and that I should be ready in time."

Thankfully, that seemed to keep her friends happy, and Sophie spent the rest of the day dreaming of what it would be like to see her dad again. When he left she had been only seven. Back then she couldn't even pronounce her *th* sounds properly, but now, not only was she four years older, but she was also a djinn. *The only djinn to have created Solomon's Elixir.*

By the time the final bell rang, Sophie was buzzing with excitement. Not least since at lunch Kara had received a text message from Malik to say that he finally had a lead on Manny and he would BITSYFC, which they had finally decided must mean *be in touch soon you funky chickens.*

Soon. It would all be okay soon.

Then she caught sight of her mom's old Toyota pulling into the parking lot and she ran over.

"You look happy," her mom said as she headed toward

Mr. Rivers's house. "And while I'd like to believe it's be-cause you're looking forward to babysitting Ryan today, I have the feeling it's something else."

"Of course I'm looking forward to babysitting Ryan," Sophie assured her mom quite truthfully; now that she could turn herself invisible, Ryan would be getting a nas-ty shock if he tried to bite her and she just disappeared. After all, if it worked at school, then it was sure to work on a six-year-old kid.

"Well, I'm pleased that at least one of my daughters is happy," her mom continued as she pulled out into the traffic and started to drive down King Avenue.

"Are you sure there's something wrong with Meg? I mean, the girl loves sharks—maybe it's just part of her weirdly gruesome nature?"

"I don't think so," her mom said as she turned left onto Meadow Lane and slowed down so that an old woman could shuffle across the street. "I tried to talk to her again after breakfast, but all she would say was that she likes things the way they are and she doesn't want anything to change."

"Yes, well, when change involves selling the house and moving to Montana, I tend to agree with her," Sophie said as she reached up and touched the lucky guitar pick that was hanging from her neck. "But some change is good change. I mean, things are okay now, but who's to say that something can't happen to make life even better?"

Sophie's mom started to smile. "Oh, honey, you've got

no idea how happy I am to hear you say that. I mean, I know I was stuck in a rut for a long time, but I've finally managed to see that sometimes good things can happen when you very least expect them to."

"Exactly." Sophie gave an empathetic nod of her head, since it was fair to say that six weeks ago she never expected to become a djinn *or* to find out the truth about her missing dad. But now, she was almost on the verge of changing their entire life. And considering the extra attention Sophie's mom was putting into her appearance, not to mention how happy she was lately, it was almost like she *knew* that Sophie's dad was on the brink of coming home.

And…but whatever Sophie was about to think next was lost as her mom pulled into Mr. Rivers's driveway and Sophie caught sight of Jonathan Tait standing outside his house next door, looking adorable in a pair of baggy jeans and Sophie's favorite apple-green hoodie, which made his golden curls look even more golden.

A happy sigh escaped her lips. Even better, the minute Jonathan saw her, his eyes widened in surprise and he started to jog over to the car. Sophie immediately wished that her flat blonde hair wasn't quite so flat.

"And actually, while we're on the subject of things changing…" Her mom stopped the car and gave an awkward cough. "There is something I wanted to talk to you about. *And you're not listening to me, are you?*"

"Huh?" Sophie blinked as she dragged her gaze away

from Jonathan for a moment and turned back to her mom. "Did you say something?"

"Never mind." Her mom shot her a rueful smile. "I know better than to try to talk to you when there's a cute boy around. Go and say hello to him, and I'll let Max know we're here."

"Thanks, Mom." Sophie pushed open the car door. "You're the best."

"I know," her mom agreed before narrowing her eyes. "Is your hair looking bouncier than normal?"

"Er, of course not. I've just been using some new conditioner." Sophie crossed her fingers as she quickly scrambled out of the car to greet Jonathan.

"Hey, Mrs. Campbell." Jonathan nodded as Sophie's mom walked toward the front of Mr. Rivers's house. Then he turned back to Sophie and smiled. "So I guess you got roped into babysitting Ryan the biter again. Ouch."

"I know. It was kind of a last-minute thing," Sophie explained, returning his smile and valiantly resisting the urge to push one of his blond curls out of his eyes. "So how was basketball?"

"It was pretty cool." Jonathan nodded. "Though if I'd known you were going to be hanging out here all afternoon, I wouldn't have arranged to go to Cooper's house to play Halo. I could've hung with you instead. Man, here he is now to pick me up."

"Maybe I'll still be here when you get back?" Sophie said in a hopeful voice, savoring the fact that Jonathan wanted to hang out with her. There were just some things that a girl never got sick of hearing.

"Sounds good to me," he agreed as he gave her one final goofy grin and hurried over to the car, where Cooper Mitchell was waiting for him. Sophie waited until he was gone before she turned and walked toward Mr. Rivers's house, a dreamy smile still on her face.

An hour later Sophie wasn't smiling quite so much. Ryan had already asked for three snacks and had made Sophie crawl on her hands and knees to look for a piece of missing LEGO—which, when she'd finally wished for it, had appeared in her hand smelling very much like the small pond at the back of the garden. Judging from the surprised (and disappointed) expression on Ryan's face, Sophie realized he must've put it there on purpose. Little beast. That's when he started throwing marbles at her.

In the end, the only way she had managed to stop him was by turning herself invisible and taking the marbles from him. That had caused him to cry so much that she had conjured up the latest Guitar Hero game for him to play with. Even then, he hadn't said thank you. But at least, judging by the noise coming from the guest room, Sophie might be able to have some time to herself.

She collapsed onto the large leather sofa. It was nothing like the lumpy one at her mom's house, which had a big stain where Meg had once spilled some ketchup, as well as shredded sides, courtesy of Mr. Jaws.

She ignored the blast of music coming from upstairs as she wondered how Malik was getting on with his lead. More importantly, she wondered how long it would be before she heard back from him. As a positive person she wanted to believe it would be within the next few minutes. Of course, as someone who had known Malik for the last six weeks, she realized it could also be considerably longer. His jaunt to France being just the latest example.

Had she mentioned how much she hated waiting? Normally she would've called Kara or Harvey, but they were both busy. And after what had happened in the basement that last time she was here, exploring the house wasn't something she was eager to do. Which left her with homework.

She reluctantly flipped open her Spanish book and was just about to start when she glanced out the window just in time to see a large white catering van pulling up the Taits' driveway. Sophie gazed at it with interest as a smart-looking woman holding a large black folder got out. She was quickly followed by a fat man with a bunch of helium balloons. They must be there about the anniversary party.

The anniversary party that *she* was going to!

Sophie grinned with excitement as she thought about the gorgeous outfit that she and Kara had spotted at the mall last week (the one that was now hanging in Sophie's closet, since that's what eleven-year-old girls with magical powers tended to do). Then she realized that, with all the excitement, she hadn't had a chance to see her dress and new shoes together. She closed her eyes and wished for them both to appear.

She grinned as they hovered in front of her like a floating mannequin. Not just because they were helping her levitation abilities, but because that last time she had been babysitting, Ryan had snuck in and stolen her good jeans, which had been the thing that had led her to release Malik accidentally from his bottle. Not something that she was—

"There you are," a voice suddenly announced, and Sophie spun around in time to see Melissa Tait standing next to the sofa. She looked as pristinely perfect as ever, with her blonde hair hanging down over one shoulder in a complicated French braid that Sophie could never hope to manage.

The floating boots immediately fell to the carpet with a soft thud, closely followed by the dress. Sophie felt her cheeks start to blaze; getting caught using magic by her arch-nemesis wasn't exactly the smartest move she'd ever made.

"M-melissa," she stammered as the buzzing sensation in her veins finally started to die away. "You're probably wondering what I'm doing with the"—*floating dress and the flying shoes?*—"outfit," she finished lamely.

"Well, for a start, I can see that you're about to make a major fashion faux pas," Melissa retorted, casting a telling eye over the dress and boots that were lying in a heap on the carpet. "I mean, the boots are cute, but the floral dress is so out of fashion that it might as well have a Myspace account. Please tell me that you're not going to wear it to my parents' anniversary party."

"Of course not. I mean, no. Definitely not," Sophie said in a rush, relieved that Melissa hadn't seemed to have noticed the little display of magic. She made a mental note always to check that the door was locked before doing anything like that again. Then she frowned as she remembered that she had locked the door when Mr. Rivers had left. "And by the way, how did you get in?"

"Key." Melissa held it up. "Mr. Rivers is letting me use his place to sort through and scan my parents' old photographs for the party. We're going to get some blown up and framed, plus make a video montage of them," she explained, walking over to an antique-looking dresser and pulling out a large cardboard box and a very pink laptop that she had obviously left here on her last visit. "Anyway, I'm glad you're here. I need to talk to you."

"Oh." Sophie's stomach plummeted as she remembered that she'd spent the better part of yesterday and today making herself invisible just to avoid this very conversation. Would it be very wrong to disappear right now? However, she didn't even bother to answer her own question. Instead, she took a deep breath. She might as well get this over and done with right now. "Look, Melissa, about those books on the Roman Empire, the thing is that—"

"Yeah, yeah, I know." Melissa held up a hand so that Sophie could see her perfectly manicured fingers, complete with purple nail polish. "I should've texted Jonathan back to say thank you. Don't worry. My precious brother has already flipped out at me about it. Not that I did it on purpose, it was just that as soon as I got the books, I bumped into Ben, and—"

"Hang on a moment." Sophie narrowed her eyes as she tried to process what the other girl was saying. "Do you mean that you actually got the books?"

"Well, yeah." Melissa gave a slight tilt of her head. "And I got the assignment done, too, which, according to Jonathan, was all because of you. No offense, but that isn't completely true—you weren't the one who had to miss *Vampire Diaries* to do it."

"Riiight." Sophie was still trying to get used to the fact that Melissa wasn't actually mad at her.

"So then Jonathan flipped out some more when I told him that I didn't apologize to you at school. Which is so unfair when I did actually wait at your stupid locker for ages, but it was like you had disappeared off the face of the earth. Plus, it's not my fault that you're such a freak that you don't even own a cell phone. I mean, seriously, what's that all about?"

"Trust me, it's not my idea," Sophie assured her, not bothering to point out that calling someone a freak wasn't always the best way to apologize. Then she narrowed her eyes and studied Melissa's perfect face. "So let me get this straight, you've been trying to say you're sorry to me because Jonathan asked you to?"

"We are twins," Melissa reminded her before reluctantly adding, "Okay, and so the other reason is that we're supposed to be doing a speech together for the anniversary party, and Jonathan refused to do it unless I said I was sorry."

"Right," Sophie said again in an uncertain voice. This wouldn't have been the first time that she'd misinterpreted something Melissa had said to her. However, instead of rolling her eyes, Melissa seemed to be... *smiling.* "Er, well, I guess that's great. Apology accepted."

"Thanks. Oh, and don't forget to tell Jonathan that I've done it," Melissa reminded her in a sharp voice. "Anyway, I'd better get to work on these photographs. I want to get them finished before Ryan decides to set fire to them or something. Wouldn't put it past the evil little so-and-so."

"You're going to stay here?" Sophie asked in surprise. "If Mr. Rivers lets you use his place, and you knew you had to do some work over here, why aren't you the one babysitting Ryan?"

"Are you serious? That kid is vile. No offense, but there isn't enough money in the world to tempt me to look after him. Yesterday he was throwing marbles at me over the fence, and he didn't stop until I threatened to have my mom run over his skateboard with her SUV."

"Snap. He was throwing marbles at me, too, until I hid them all from him," Sophie said, not bothering to add that she'd used her magic to do so.

"You did? Nice. I didn't think you had it in you." Melissa nodded her head in approval as she smiled. Then Sophie blinked. Had she somehow ended up in an alternate universe or something? Melissa Tait was smiling at her. Maybe it was another djinn thing that Malik had forgotten to mention? But before she could figure it out Melissa coughed. "Actually, if you're not doing anything, you could help me sort through these photographs. It's such a nightmare, and of course they didn't have digital cameras back then, so everything needs to be scanned in. It's prehistoric."

"Er, sure." Sophie cautiously nodded her head. She had no idea why Melissa was suddenly being so nice to her, but, like everyone at Robert Robertson Middle School knew, it was better to have Melissa as a friend than as an enemy.

10

"ARE YOU SURE THAT YOU'RE FEELING OKAY?" HARVEY asked on Thursday afternoon as they crowded into Sophie's bedroom. The minute they shut the door behind them, Sophie conjured up a packet of Oreos and three cans of Diet Coke, while making a mental note to hide the trash from her mom.

"Yeah, because I've heard that prolonged exposure to Melissa Tait can make you break out in hives," Kara chimed in from where she was sitting cross-legged on Sophie's yellow-and-white comforter, hugging a shopping bag to her chest.

"I'm talking about whether Sophie's had any aftereffects from all the flying she did yesterday," Harvey corrected her as he reached for a cookie and started to pull it apart, which was his preferred way of eating them.

"And I'm talking about the fact that Melissa can't be trusted, so if she was nice to Sophie, then it was for a reason. Oh, and did you see her today at school? All that smiling and waving? Something's definitely going on."

Kara folded her arms and poked out her lower lip.

"Guys, nothing's going on, and weirdly enough, Melissa was actually being quite nice," Sophie assured them while letting out a silent groan. Despite the fact that she had already explained what had happened at Mr. Rivers's house yesterday afternoon, her friends had been quizzing her about it all day. Which was why Sophie didn't bother to add that she'd actually enjoyed looking at the wedding photographs. It was obvious where Melissa got her fashion sense from, since her mom had been wearing an amazing ivory silk dress that nipped into a tiny waist and had about a zillion tiny beads sewn onto the bodice.

It had taken almost an hour to sort through everything, and once they were finished, Melissa had let her look at a bunch of photos from various family vacations. Sophie had immediately honed in on Jonathan, though she couldn't help but notice how normal Melissa looked in them. There were even a couple where she was making a face, which was pretty funny.

Jonathan was always telling her that his twin sister wasn't so bad, and while Sophie had wanted to believe him, Melissa's personality had always gotten in the way. But after yesterday she was starting to wonder if he had a point. Then she caught sight of Kara's face and realized that no matter what she might think, she wasn't going to change her friend's mind anytime soon.

"But enough about me, I want to see what you got at the mall yesterday afternoon. You're going to look so amazing when you go to the movies. Patrick won't know what hit him."

"Actually"—Kara bowed her head and started to fiddle with the shopping bag in her lap—"I'm not sure I'm going to go."

"What?" Sophie shot her friend a perplexed look; it was like Kara had turned into a different person since Patrick had asked her out. "What are you talking about? I thought we discussed this. I mean, you like him and he likes you. Am I missing something?"

Kara didn't answer, and finally Harvey let out a sigh. "Kara had an 'incident' yesterday at the mall," he explained. "Her mom had gone to pick up some dry cleaning, and while she was away, Kara saw Patrick in the food court."

"You did? What happened? Why didn't you tell me about it today at school?"

"I think she was too traumatized. Apparently, it was another *mwhooahwwh* moment," Harvey said.

"It was way worse than what happened the other day." Kara let out a wail, her cheeks both bright red. "It was awful. I was completely incapable of speech. There might even have been some snorting."

"I'm sure it wasn't that bad," Sophie instantly reassured her. "Besides, I've known you forever, and I've never heard you snort. Not even when we all went to see *Shrek* and laughed our butts off."

"Okay, so maybe there wasn't snorting," Kara conceded. "But there was definitely moronic muteness. It's hopeless. I can't go to the movies with him if I can't even talk to him. Why is this so hard for me? I feel like my brain has been taken over by aliens."

Honestly, Sophie had no idea. Sure, she got nervous when she spoke to Jonathan but never at the expense of her vocal chords. However, there was no way she was going to tell Kara this. Instead, she gave her friend a reassuring smile.

"Of course it's not hopeless. And this is something we can fix. You just need to start talking about stuff he's interested in. That will give you time to relax instead of freezing up. We can work out a list of discussion topics. It will be like an assignment!"

"But I don't know what he's interested in because I can never get the words out to ask him. I told you, it's hopeless." Kara's bottom lip was wobbling now, and Harvey inched back a bit, obviously worried that tears might be next.

"Oh." Sophie paused for a moment before widening her eyes. "I've got it! What if tomorrow at lunchtime I turn myself invisible and follow Patrick around? Then I can see what he does and what he talks about. I could even find out what library books he's reading. Then we can work on a list for you."

Kara was silent for a moment before she slowly nodded

her head. "Then, even if I freaked out while we were talk-ing about one thing, I would have something else I could move on to."

"Exactly." Sophie grinned as she reached over and squeezed her friend's hand. Then she nodded at the shop-ping bags, which were the whole reason why they had arranged to meet at Sophie's house after school. "So am I finally going to see this outfit? The waiting is killing me."

"I guess so." Kara started to brighten as she reverently opened up the bag and pulled out a gorgeous pair of red skinny jeans and a black-and-white T-shirt with some kind of modern art painting on it. "And thanks. I feel loads better now."

"Hey, that's what having a positive-thinking friend is all about," Sophie said as she leaned over and inspected her friend's new clothes. Then she looked up and smiled. "These are gorgeous. You will look amazing. And if you like, you could borrow that black jacket of mine. It's in the closet if you want to take it home and try it out."

"Are you serious?" Kara instantly jumped to her feet, hurried over to the closet, and started to rum-mage through it. "You know how much I love that jacket and . . . hey, where did you get this?"

"Get what?" Sophie stopped inspecting Kara's new T-shirt and looked up to where her friend was holding a turquoise-colored silky dress that nipped in at the waist before falling down to three inches above the knee. Look-ing at it again instantly made her smile, and she jumped to her feet. "Oh, yeah. Isn't it amazing? I was just about to show it to you. I conjured it up. Do you like it?"

"Um, yeah. I mean, it's gorgeous," Kara agreed as she held it up so she could study it better. "But what's it for? I thought you had a new policy of not conjuring up more stuff than you needed in case your mom did a random closet inspection."

"I'm going to wear it to the party," Sophie explained as she took the dress from her friend so she could hold it against herself as she did several clumsy pirouettes around the room.

"The party?" Kara looked confused as she turned back to the closet and started to flick through the rack. "But what about your other outfit? I thought you'd decided on the floral skirt and the shrug that we saw at the mall the other day? You said you already zapped it up."

"I had, and I really thought it was perfect." Sophie stopped her twirling and sat back down on the bed, still lovingly clutching her new dress. "But then I realized that it made me look short."

"You are short," Harvey reminded her.

"Thanks, Sherlock." Sophie rolled her eyes at him. "But the thing is that Melissa says that short girls should never wear floral dresses and shrugs. Apparently, it's some kind of designer golden rule. She said it would be perfect if I was as tall as Taylor Swift, but for someone my height, it would make me look even shorter. In fact, I can't believe I didn't realize it sooner. Anyway, she pulled a copy of

*Girl2day* out of her purse and suggested I try something like this, so I did and you know what? She was so right. Can you believe it?"

"Not really," Kara admitted. "You loved that outfit. You said it was amazing."

"Yes, but it was *short* amazing. This new dress is *tall* amazing," Sophie explained. Besides, it was all right for Kara, who looked fantastic in whatever she wore, but when you were height challenged like Sophie was, it wasn't quite so simple. In fact, when Sophie had first become a djinn, she had actually tried to make herself taller, before Malik told her that she could try all she wanted but it wouldn't make a difference. The best she could do was to create an illusion of tallness, and that wouldn't be happening for another three hundred years at least. Which was why, when she found a dress that gave her the appearance of an extra inch, she was going to take it.

But despite this, Kara's lips still pursed, which was odd since, apart from the occasional burst of stubbornness, Kara was never normally prickly. Sophie narrowed her eyes. "Is this because Melissa helped me choose it?"

"Of course not." Kara shook her head and let out a sigh. "Okay, maybe. Ignore me, I just wish that you had been hanging with me when Patrick had turned up rather than talking about clothes with Melissa Tait."

"I told you, the only reason I was there was because my mom made me babysit. I would've much rather been at the mall with you," Sophie assured her friend before shooting her a hopeful look. "So are we cool?"

"Of course we are." Kara instantly gave a watery sniff. "I was just being a doofus."

"No, you weren't. If anyone was being a doofus, I was," Sophie countered.

"Well, personally, I think the pair of you are pretty doofy to be worried over a dress," Harvey pointed out, but before either of the girls could comment Malik appeared in the middle of the room. Today he was wearing a black T-shirt and gray trousers, and his Zac-like hair was spiked up like a hedgehog.

But Sophie hardly noticed. Instead, her heart started to hammer in her chest as she jumped to her feet, causing the turquoise dress to fall into a heap on the floor. She ignored it as she clutched her hands together and stared at him.

"So? How did it go? Did you find anything out?"

"Oh, yes, I most certainly did," Malik announced as he made his way over to Sophie's bookshelf and produced a packet of M&M's from behind her collection of books on positive thinking. "And I would've told you about it sooner if I could've found you. I mean, seriously, I was looking everywhere for you yesterday. I even tried the school auditorium, and you have no idea how much of a racket they were making in there. Where have you been?"

"I was babysitting at Mr. Rivers's house, but I was home by six."

"Mr. Rivers's house?" Malik was immediately distracted as he paused from ripping open the M&M's with his teeth. "As in the basement where I was stuck in an ugly red vase for what seemed like an eternity? That place is evil."

"That's exactly what we tried to tell her," Harvey added.

"*And* she had to spend all afternoon with Melissa 'she thinks she's so great' Tait," Kara chimed in.

"Look, like I told Kara and Harvey, Mr. Rivers is fine. He's actually been really kind to my mom lately, especially with her pottery business."

"Oh, and I haven't?" Malik wanted to know. "I mean, the other day on Facebook your mom wanted to know if she should cook hamburgers or pasta, and I totally helped her."

Sophie blinked at him for a moment before deciding that it was better to just ignore that last statement.

"Okay, back to my dad. How did it go?" she asked as she tried not to focus on the way her pulse was wildly fluttering.

"Well, my young friends, I finally managed to catch up with Manny the Moody, in a very unsavory bar, and let's just say that he's not what I would call the most congenial of djinns. *However*," he quickly added, obviously catching Sophie's frustrated expression, "the important thing is that he's a talker, and in half an hour he told me everything we need to know."

"Really?" Sophie's hands felt clammy as she let go of the breath that she hadn't known she was holding. "You've really found him?"

"I really found him," Malik confirmed with a nod of his head. "I'm not going to say that it was easy. Or cheap—if a certain camel loses in next month's All Sahara Invitational Challenge, then there's going to be one cranky djinn."

"So tell me everything. Has Manny seen my dad? Is he okay? What is he bound to? Will it be hard for us to find him?" Sophie inquired as a bubble of happiness started to swell up inside her. Being a positive thinker, she had always known that this moment would arrive, but she hadn't expected it to feel quite so... amazing.

"Last time Manny saw your dad was a year ago, and apparently, he was fine. A bit weak in strength since most sahirs tend to overwork their djinns. He also told me that Sheterum is a rabid art collector, and it gives him a sick pleasure to bind his djinns into various paintings when he's not making them work for him. Manny himself was stuck in a miniature Degas for over a hundred years. If you could see the size of him, you would appreciate the irony."

"And what about Sophie's dad?" Harvey wanted to know. "Did this Manny know what painting he's in?"

"He did. This is the pride of his collection, and since Sophie's father is Sheterum's prized djinn, it's no surprise that he's bound to it." Malik nodded as he pulled a photograph out of his back pocket and passed it over to her.

Sophie caught her breath and tried to ignore her trembling hands as she studied the photograph. It was a rainbow splat of swirling colors and geometric shapes, somehow all existing side by side in random neatness. Honestly, it looked like something that her younger sister might've done. Not that she cared what it looked like; the main thing was that she now knew exactly where her dad was and what she had to do to release him. A burst of happiness went racing through her as Kara leaned over her shoulder to study it.

"Whoa. Sophie, that's a Kandinsky." Kara breathed in awe as she reached out and reverently touched the photograph. "I mean, that's a seriously famous painting that your dad is bound to. That's amazing, and"—she stopped abruptly, probably after catching Harvey's pointed look—"very important because we now know where to find him."

"That's right," Malik agreed as he pulled out a roll of paper and flattened it. From where Sophie was standing, it looked like the floor plans to Sheterum's mansion. "According to Manny, our best plan is to fly directly into the room. He's given me a photograph so that you can visualize where to land. If we get it right and land in between the sensors for the security system, then no alarms will be triggered until we're ready to make our move. Then we'll have about a minute. Oh, and he also mentioned brain-pulverizing laser beams. Typical sahir stunt. They do love to pulverize things."

As he spoke, Harvey and Kara began to pore over the plans, but Sophie just stood perfectly still as her fingers traced a line along the photograph of the painting her father was trapped in.

She felt like she had been doing a jigsaw puzzle and that the final pieces had just fallen into place. She had everything she needed to rescue her dad. The picture he was bound to, the floor plans of the mansion, the day that Sheterum would be away, and most importantly, Solomon's Elixir.

She allowed herself a smile.

Soon they would be a family again. Sophie had only to close her eyes to see the four of them sitting around the large teak dining room table, eating the lasagna that her dad was so famous for making, laughing, and joking at the various things that had happened during the day. A family once again.

11

OKAY, SO THIS WOULD WORK A LOT BETTER IF YOU could stop smiling so much," Malik complained half an hour later as he glared at where Sophie was sitting with her legs crossed in the middle of the red-and-purple carpet, which was currently spread out in the back garden. "You have to understand that flying a carpet has a certain element of coolness attached to it, which is completely lost if you go around looking like the dorky girl who has just won a free day trip to Disneyland."

"Sorry. No more smiling," Sophie assured him with a smile. She put her hand over her mouth to try to hide her happiness, but it was hard now that they were so close to rescuing her dad. She smiled again, and Malik made a snorting noise.

"I knew we should've taken this practice session down to the basement. I bet you wouldn't be smiling then. Plus, it would let us get away from your sister's cat. I tell you, that stupid thing is really starting to get on my nerves. Before you got home from school, I was up in your room innocently checking my Facebook account when it *launched* itself at me like I was some kind of heinous criminal."

Sophie groaned. Despite her best efforts to bribe him with Pretty Kitty snacks, Mr. Jaws had taken to hissing and growling every time she or Malik was in the room. But still, she would rather face Mr. Jaws than all the spiders in the basement, so she decided that she had better not annoy Malik anymore.

"I promise, no more smiling while I'm on the carpet. I will be the model of concentration. Okay?"

"Humph," Malik grunted as he launched into a big lecture on jumping through time and space. Most of it was filled with words that she didn't understand. When he was finished, Sophie almost thought he was going to make her jump into the basement like the other day, but instead he announced that she could try going to the school. "And," he suddenly added, "I think this time you can fly solo. You've still got the stabilizers on, but you won't have me with you. Do you feel ready?"

Yes. No. Maybe. But instead Sophie nodded her head; until she mastered her flying, she couldn't see her dad.

"I'm ready," she said in a firm voice. She closed her eyes and blocked everything out until the only thing she was conscious of was the hallway at school where her locker was. Thankfully, considering that was the place where Jonathan had first talked to her, it was something she had visualized on a regular basis. Then she pictured a plastic bubble all around her and the carpet before finally blinking her eyes three times.

She felt a familiar tug in her stomach, and when she opened her eyes, she was really in the hallway of the school. She was just about to congratulate herself when she suddenly heard a loud noise and looked up to see the janitor pushing some kind of huge floor polishing machine toward her.

For a moment Sophie just stared at it, assuming he would stop for her, before remembering that the janitor couldn't see her. Panic raced through her—she had a funny feeling that if he ran over her, she would feel it. But she felt frozen, unable to think or move, and suddenly, she understood just why Malik had been so pedantic in his teachings. Her heart pounded, but just as the polisher reached the tip of her carpet, she snapped out of it and quickly pictured her backyard. A second later relief flooded through her as she was once again in her garden, her carpet hovering three feet off the ground.

Sophie let out a grateful sigh, and for a moment she lay back on the carpet to try to regain her composure. That was far too close. But before her heart rate had a chance to return to normal she heard a yowling noise and sat up just in time to see Mr. Jaws launch himself at the corner of the carpet. The impact caused the whole thing to start wobbling, and it took all of Sophie's skills to bring it down to the ground without falling off.

Then she looked over to see Mr. Jaws hunched on all fours, his eyes narrow and his tail fluffy, like he was going to pounce all over again.

"Seriously. What's his problem? It's almost like he's never seen an invisible person fly on an invisible carpet before." Malik floated over and glared at the cat, but the sound of his voice seemed only to aggravate Mr. Jaws even more. "Still, at least it's stopped you smiling so much."

"How can he even tell that I'm here?" Sophie demanded as Malik's words reminded her that she was still invisible. "Do you think it's a djinn thing?"

"More like a stupid dumb animal thing," Malik retorted. "Anyway, if you can't get rid of that cat, then I might as well go. Even being in the same backyard as that thing is giving me the creeps."

"No, you stay right here," Sophie said in alarm as she thought of how she'd almost frozen when the janitor and the polishing machine had been coming toward her. She needed a lot more practice, and if Malik disappeared, then she would be stuck. She lunged at the cat, but before she could get him, he darted away and hurled himself underneath her mom's pottery shed. Sophie got on her belly and poked her head under there, but Mr. Jaws edged farther away from her.

"I don't think it's working," Malik announced unnecessarily, his head suddenly appearing down the other end of the shed. "Cats aren't just stupid, they're very belligerent, too. Try turning visible."

"What?" Sophie spluttered, before realizing that his suggestion was actually a really good idea. She clicked her fingers and said the word *visible*. At the sight of her, the cat promptly shed about three bucketfuls of fur all over her as he violently tried to dart past her. But Sophie lunged for him again, and this time she made sure that he couldn't wriggle out of her grip.

Mr. Jaws yowled even louder, but Sophie ignored the noise as she marched inside the house and up to Meg's bedroom. Her sister's door was open, and Meg was sitting in the middle of the floor surrounded by old *National Geographic* magazines that she was cutting shark pictures out of with her child-friendly scissors.

"Hey, if I'm not allowed to go into your room, then how come you can come into mine?" Meg demanded in a sulky voice.

"Because your cat's driving me crazy," Sophie retorted, not bothering to add that he was also ruining her flying practice. Instead, she dropped Mr. Jaws onto Meg's bright blue comforter. The cat immediately darted into Meg's lap.

"Well, you still shouldn't be here. I have rights, too, you know." Meg poked out her lower lip, and suddenly Sophie remembered that she had promised her mom she would try to learn what was bothering her sister—apart from the fact that she was friendly with a crazy cat. Sophie joined her sister on the floor and picked up one of the shark pictures her sister had been cutting out.

"Look, Meggy. Mom's totally worried about you right now. What's going on?" Sophie asked. She glanced at the picture in her hands and noticed the shark's bloodstained teeth. She immediately put it back down.

Meg sniffed as she patted Mr. Jaws's fur. "Why do you care? You're too busy doing your own stuff."

"Of course I'm not too busy," Sophie protested as she glanced at her watch, hoping that Malik was still waiting for her.

"Yes, you are," Meg retorted in a stubborn voice that Sophie was only too familiar with.

"Is this about Mom trying to sell the house?" Sophie wrinkled her nose. "Because you know that she's changed her mind about that. We're not going anywhere. You should be happy."

"I'm never going to be happy again," Meg announced in a dramatic voice before turning her attention back to her shark pictures and letting out a long sigh. Instinctively, Sophie reached over and squeezed her sister's hand and gave her a small nudge.

"I bet you will." Sophie beamed, still not quite able to contain her happiness. "In fact, I can guarantee it." However, when Meg's pout didn't show any sign of disappearing, Sophie leaned forward and lowered her voice. "Okay, what if I tell you a secret? Will that make you feel better?"

"What kind of secret?" Meg demanded in a noncommittal voice.

"Like the fact that I might have some good news about Dad."

"W-what?" Meg instantly gave Sophie her full attention, her navy eyes bright as stars.

"The thing is that you can't tell anyone, okay." Sophie suddenly realized that it might not be the cleverest idea to tell a six-year-old a secret. "You have to pinky promise."

Meg immediately stuck out her pinky and hooked it onto Sophie's. Then she said in a small voice, "You know where Dad is? Does Mom know?"

Sophie shook her head, unable to hide her smile any longer. "No and I shouldn't have said anything to you in case I'm wrong. But you just looked so sad. The thing is, Meggy, hopefully, he'll be back with us soon and we'll be a proper family again."

"Will he be here before tomorrow night?" Meg asked. Sophie blinked in surprise. That wasn't exactly the answer she had been expecting.

"Okay, so it won't be quite that fast, but it should be soon." She reached out to squeeze Meg's hand again, and Mr. Jaws swiped a paw at her. She pulled her hand back and then frowned. "Anyway, what's so special about Friday night?"

"That's when Mom's going out on a date with Mr. Rivers, so if Daddy's going to come home, it would be better to do it before then," Meg elaborated.

"What?" Sophie's jaw dropped in surprise. "Since when?"

"Since I heard her talking on the phone to get Mrs. Corbett to be our sitter," Meg replied.

"That's it?" Sophie let out a long groan as her heart rate returned to a more even pace. Talk about scaring her over nothing. "Maybe Mom wants to go to a movie or something? Because I can assure you that there's no way she's going on a date. Especially not with Mr. Rivers. He's just been helping out with her pottery business. They're friends," Sophie explained. But Meg just shook her head, causing Mr. Jaws to jump out of her lap and hurl himself across the room.

"It's a date," Meg said in a petulant voice. "And it's not fair, because I don't want Mr. Rivers to be our new dad."

"Of course he's not going to be our new dad." Sophie rolled her eyes as she got to her feet. Even though her younger sister often had the uncanny knack of knowing things first, she had definitely gotten her wires crossed this time. "In fact, let's go find Mom right now so that she can tell you for herself that she isn't going on a date with anyone. *Mom*," she called out as she and Meg stepped into the hallway. "Mom, where are you?"

"I'm in my bedroom," their mom replied as they both hurried in, just in time to see her checking her reflection in the mirror. She wore a fitted red dress that Sophie had never seen before. Sophie also noticed that there were a lot of shopping bags littered all over the large bed in the center of the room. "What's up?"

"Meg has this crazy idea that you're going on a date with Mr. Rivers. I think that's what she's been worried about—" Sophie started to say before she remembered that not only had her mom gone shopping, but she had recently gotten her hair cut. Suddenly Sophie had a very bad feeling; she sat down on the edge of the bed and tried to ignore the way her heart was hammering in her chest. It was like someone was trying to squeeze all the air out of her body. *"M-mom?"*

Her mom bit into her lower lip and moved some of the shopping bags off the bed so that she could sit down next to her. "I am. I was going to tell you yesterday, but then you got distracted by Jonathan. I know we've talked about it a bit, but—"

"What?" Sophie managed to break out of her daze for a moment. "We never talked about you going on a date with Mr. Rivers. Trust me, it's the kind of thing I would've remembered."

"Yes, we did. When we were down in the basement. We talked about moving on to a new chapter and putting the past behind us." Her mom looked confused.

"I didn't mean you should move on and date anyone," Sophie yelped. "I was talking about . . . well, I wasn't talking about that! How could you even think that's what I meant?"

"Honey, I'm sorry if there's been a misunderstanding, but I don't see why you're so upset. It's been four years.

What do you want me to do? Sit at home on my own every night like I've been doing?"

"Yes, absolutely." Sophie nodded, an edge of desperation starting to seep into her voice as she shot her mom a pleading look. "You can't go out with him. Please, Mom. You really can't."

"Besides," Meg suddenly decided to chime in, "Sophie told me that Daddy's coming home, and so you don't need to go on a date with Mr. Rivers. You can just go on a date with Daddy instead."

Sophie widened her eyes and stared at her sister in horror. Which bit of "don't tell anyone" had she not understood? Not to mention the whole pinky promise ritual. Unfortunately, it was too late, and Sophie winced in dismay at the way her mom was frowning.

"Meg," their mom said in a tight voice, "could you please go to your room for a moment? I need to talk to Sophie."

Meg might sometimes be a bit clueless, but even she could see the way their mom's face had hardened, and she quickly raced out of the room without a word. Great, so now she showed some restraint. The minute her sister was gone, Sophie's mom turned to her, brown eyes narrowed and jaw clenched.

"Sophie Campbell, I can't believe you would tell your six-year-old sister that her father might be coming home."

"But—" Sophie started to say. Her mom held up her hand and shook her head.

"I think you've done enough talking for a while. I know how much you love and miss him, and so do I, but we've already been through this. Your dad's left us, and he's not coming back. I'm sorry that you're upset about it, but I've made up my mind about this. Tomorrow night I'm going out on a date."

12

A DATE. HER MOM WAS GOING ON A DATE. WITH someone who wasn't Sophie's dad.

How could this be happening? And why now? Especially considering how far she'd come. After all, it hadn't been exactly easy to get an interview with the Djinn Council and to find the recipe to make Solomon's Elixir. And don't even get her started on learning how to fly and getting the floor plans for Sheterum's mansion. For what? So that her mom could go on a date with someone else a week before Sophie was finally due to rescue her dad?

Suddenly she understood what the phrase "a day late and a dollar short" really meant.

It was like the Universe hated her or something. But that couldn't be right because she and the Universe were as one. Not to mention the fact that she had been doing affirmations for the last four years to make sure that they would once again be a happy family. *And nowhere in those affirmations had there been any mention of Mr. Rivers.*

Just thinking about it caused Sophie's heart to start

pounding an anxious rhythm. It was such a disaster. And even worse, so far she hadn't been able to stop it. Though it wasn't from a lack of trying. She had given her mom some excellent reasons why she couldn't go out on a date (ranging from the way he folded the towels in the guest bathroom to the fact that he was related to the evil Ryan the biter), but so far her mom had absolutely refused to change her mind about it.

In the past, Sophie had always thought that Meg was the stubborn one in the family, but since last night, it was becoming increasingly obvious who her sister had inherited the stubborn gene from. Oh, and to make matters worse, after giving her another lecture on how bad it was to fill her sister's head with fairy tales, her mom had decided to give Sophie extra chores around the house for two weeks. And yes, technically, Sophie could use her magic to do them, but that was hardly the point. After all, Meg didn't get extra chores, and she was the one who had broken her promise—

"Hello there." Harvey's hand suddenly appeared in front of her as the lunch bell finally rang. Kara had been excused for some special *Wizard of Oz* meeting, so they were going to catch up with her in the cafeteria. All around her students were talking and pouring out toward the exit like a tidal wave. She reluctantly joined the flow as Harvey shot her a quizzical look. "Is everything okay?"

"You mean apart from the fact that my mom's going on a date tonight with the horrible guy who kept poor Malik ruthlessly locked up in his basement for a gazillion years, and I *still* haven't figured out a way to stop it yet," Sophie asked as they squeezed their way through the crowds.

"I thought that was an accident. Didn't you say that he didn't know Malik was in the vase?" Harvey scratched his chin in confusion. "Not to mention the fact that you said how nice it was that he was helping your mom with her pottery business."

"Yes, but that was before he decided to ask my mom out and in turn try to ruin our lives," Sophie retorted darkly. "Now I totally hate him again. Plus, you were the one who told me that he had weird body language."

"Trust me, I know how stinky it is when parents don't stay together." Harvey gave her a nod of sympathy. "But Soph, I'm sure you will think of something. After all, that's what you do. You give it all your attention and focus, and then suddenly you and that Universe of yours figure it out."

"But what if it doesn't work this time?" Sophie tried to keep the panic out of her voice. "What if all of my luck has run out?"

"A wise friend of mine who is a great believer in positive thinking will probably tell you that luck doesn't work like that," Harvey said with a grin, and Sophie suddenly felt a bit better.

"Thanks, Har—" she started to say. But before she could finish, Malik suddenly appeared, his normally perfectly groomed Zac hair sticking out in all directions, and his crumpled *American Idol* T-shirt covered in Cheetos crumbs.

"What are you doing here?" Sophie demanded in a low voice, since Malik's presence at Robert Robertson Middle School seldom ended well.

"I've got some good news," he announced in a dramatic voice.

"You do?" Sophie felt her heart pound with nerves. "Is it about my dad? Do you think we can go and rescue him today? Because seriously, Malik, that would solve everything."

"It would also be insanity," Malik assured her. "It's going to be hard enough to get past Sheterum's defenses when he's away, but it will be impossible when he's at home."

"Oh." Disappointment stung as she let out a sigh. "So what is this news then?"

"I've only gone and figured out the perfect way to stop your mother from going out on a date with *that man*."

"What is it?" Sophie was instantly alert, since it turned out that Malik had been just as upset about her mom going on a date as Sophie and Meg, and he had promised that he would do all he could to stop it. He was obviously being true to his word. For once.

"We just need to tell her he's a nose picker. When I was trapped in his basement, I saw him go in there on at least three occasions, and don't even get me started on where he wiped it."

"Ew, gross." Sophie gave a delicate shudder. "That's disgusting."

"I know," Malik agreed with a fierce nod. "I mean, there's no way she can go out with him after she hears that."

"Yes, but I can't exactly tell her," Sophie reminded him. "Since she might have a few problems believing that my ghostly djinn guide, who had been trapped in a vase at the time, actually saw Mr. Rivers picking his nose—"

"And wiping it," Malik reminded her.

"And wiping it," Sophie repeated. "But the problem is, if we go down the djinn path she might ground me *forever*, and then it would be even harder to go rescue my dad. Besides, Harvey has helped me remember that it's pointless to be upset about it because the Universe will come through for us."

"Yes, well, that's easy for you to say because you're both young and naive and probably don't feel things as much as I do." Malik glumly sighed. "I mean, you think that you know someone, and then this happens. Because seriously, it's one thing for her to like your father, Tariq the Awesome, since not only is he a fine figure of a djinn, but they were actually married. But for your mom to want to go out with the likes of Max Rivers? I'm not going to lie to you, it feels like a stab in the heart."

"Er, you're a ghost, which means that, technically, you don't have a heart," Harvey pointed out in a reasonable voice as he and Sophie exchanged grins. However, a second later Harvey stopped smiling as he realized that Sophie was turning in the direction of her locker. He looked at her in alarm. "You want to go to your locker now? But it's Nacho Friday, and if we don't get there early, all the guacamole will be gone."

"And that's a bad thing?" Sophie raised an eyebrow before giving him a little push. "Anyway, you go ahead and I'll meet you there. I just need to look for my homework. I was sure I put it in my black folder, but it's not there. I blame my mom—if she hadn't dropped the dating bombshell on me, then I wouldn't have been so distracted." It was extra annoying because it wasn't even like she could conjure up another one, since for some reason her djinn magic didn't work well on homework, which, if you asked her, was a real flaw.

"Are you sure you don't mind?" Harvey asked.

"It's nachos. Who cares if she minds or not? Let's get going already," Malik said as he began to float toward the cafeteria without so much as a backward glance.

"Go. Besides, Kara's probably waiting in there," Sophie said to Harvey, and then watched him hurry away with his long, lanky strides. Once he was gone, she made her way to her locker and let out a huge sigh of relief when she found her math homework crammed into the back of her Spanish book. She had obviously been more distracted than she had realized.

However, she was feeling a lot better now that Harvey had reminded her how pointless it was to worry. Of course she would figure out a way to stop her mom from dating Mr. Rivers. And then next Friday her dad would be home, and she would never have to think about any of this stuff again.

She quickly shut her locker and was about to head to the cafeteria when she caught sight of Jonathan walking up to her, looking as goldenly glorious as ever. Suddenly all of her worries faded away.

"Hey." He came to a halt and shot her one of those dazzling smiles that made Sophie's knees knock.

"Hey," she said back to him while cursing herself for forgetting to bounce up her flat hair. Thankfully, he didn't seem to notice. Instead, he leaned against one of the lockers.

"So I was hoping I would see you today. I feel bad that I had to bail on Wednesday afternoon when you were at Mr. Rivers's house. Melissa said that you totally survived the Ryan the biter experience. That's seriously impressive stuff."

"Yeah, well, to be honest, I think he was more scared of Melissa than he was of me," Sophie confessed as she casually reached up to her hair and futilely tried to tease it with her fingers. It remained stubbornly flat.

"She can be pretty scary," he agreed. "Though it sounds like you both got on okay, because when she was telling me about how you helped her, she didn't roll her eyes or make a snorting noise once. Are you sure you didn't use magic on her?"

*Actually,* Sophie admitted to herself, *she* had *tried magic on Melissa on more than one occasion, and each time it had been a disaster.* Not that she was going to tell Jonathan that. Though perhaps once her dad was home, she would ask him if he thought she should let Jonathan in on her secret. Instead, she just shrugged. "I think she just enjoyed showing me all of your family photographs."

Jonathan raised his eyebrows in alarm. "What? I thought it was wedding photographs. Please tell me that there weren't any of the camping trip we took when I was six?"

"Do you mean the one where you tied a scarf around your waist and you were pretending it was your tail?" Sophie asked in an innocent voice before grinning. "Or the one where you—"

"Okay, stop." Jonathan's face went bright red. "This is the most embarrassing moment of my life. I'm *so* going to kill my sister for this."

"Actually, I thought they were adorable," she confessed.

"That's debatable." Jonathan shuddered and glanced at his watch. "Anyway, I'd better get over to the court, or Coach will flip."

"Cool. I've got to get to the cafeteria," Sophie said, conscious that she hadn't spent as much time with her friends as she normally did. She was just about to head there when she caught sight of Melissa Tait hurrying toward her. She was wearing a cute skirt, a simple T-shirt, and a wide belt. However, her pristine look was marred by the worried expression on her face.

"Please tell me that Jonathan's here. I really need to speak to him."

"H-he just left. I think he had practice," Sophie answered in a cautious voice; despite what had happened yesterday at Mr. Rivers's house, she didn't exactly trust Jonathan's sister. Then she noticed that Melissa's normally perfect nails were chewed to the quick. If Harvey was here, she was pretty sure he would say that Melissa was stressed. Which was crazy, since as far as Sophie knew, Melissa Tait didn't stress about anything. Did she? "Um, is everything okay?"

"No, everything's most definitely not okay," Melissa snapped. "I'm having a total crisis. I just heard back from the picture-framing guy, and he's told me that he can't get the beautiful Baroque Bronze beveled frame that I selected because there's a transport strike and it's stuck in a warehouse in New York. And get a load of this, the best he can do for me is Rustic Barnwood. I mean, do I look like a girl who would ever choose Rustic Barnwood?"

"Er, no," Sophie offered up, not really sure what Rustic Barnwood or Baroque Bronze beveled frames were. However, this seemed to please Melissa.

"Exactly. It's just so unbelievable. That's why I need to see Jonathan to decide what we should do, but of course he's not here, which is just so typical of him. And you know what? Even if he was here, he would probably just wriggle out and say that it doesn't matter if we use any old frame."

"Oh, I see." Sophie nodded, still not really sure what was going on.

"But of course it does matter," Melissa continued as she shook her blonde hair, causing it to shimmer like a waterfall. "I mean, not only is it their bronze wedding anniversary—not their rustic barnwood wedding anniversary—but our mom runs an art gallery, so she's a frame expert and if we get her an ugly one, it's like we're saying that we don't care. The frame is a symbol of how important this party is, but for some reason no one else seems to understand that." As she spoke she glared over to where the Tait-bots were all collectively waiting for her.

"Actually," Sophie found herself saying, as she thought of her own parents and how she would do literally anything to get them back together, "I know what you mean."

For a moment Melissa stopped her lip chewing. "You do?"

Sophie tightened her grip on her djinn before she nodded. "You want them to know how much you love your family and how important they are to you."

"Exactly," Melissa said, her voice laced with surprise. "And thanks. I was starting to think I was going a bit crazy. Plus, you know what's really annoying? I spent hours and hours choosing that frame. It's *the* frame, and unless there's some miracle, then I won't be able to get it."

For a moment Sophie was silent. She might not understand the big deal about getting the perfect frame, but she did understand the big deal about being with your family. Plus, if it would make Melissa happy, it would make Jonathan happy.

"Do you have a picture of this fancy-pants frame of yours?" she finally asked.

"Sure." Melissa looked surprised before she opened her purse and pulled out an expensive-looking brochure and pointed to a lavish-looking bronze frame, which had ornate moldings all the way around it. Then she pointed to a very plain unpainted wooden frame and pulled a face, leaving Sophie with no doubt that it was the alternative. Sophie quickly caught the name of the framer that was printed at the bottom of the brochure before Melissa thrust it back into her purse. "Sorry, but I can't look at it too long or it will just upset me again."

"But since the party isn't until a week from Sunday, there might still be time for the frames to come," Sophie said in a positive voice before she closed her eyes and wished for the frames to arrive.

"Well, the framer said that unless they come in today, he wouldn't have enough time to—" The rest of her words were cut off by the sound of a cell phone. Melissa immediately pulled her phone out and studied the screen, then looked at Sophie in astonishment. "You're never going to believe it, but—"

"The frames arrived?" Sophie asked, trying to fight back a smile.

"Yeah. Jonathan said that you were into all of that positive-thinking business. Maybe there's something to it after all," Melissa said. "Anyway, I'd better go and call this framer and make sure that he doesn't get any funny ideas with the color of the backing plates. But hey, thanks for listening."

"Sure," Sophie said, and then waved good-bye, still trying to get used to the new and infinitely less scary Melissa. She hurried toward the cafeteria just in time to see the red-faced lunch ladies pulling out the empty silver trays. She had no idea that she'd been talking to Melissa for so long. She glanced around the half-empty room until she caught sight of Kara and Harvey at one of the back tables.

"I'm so sorry I'm late." She dropped into the closest seat and pulled out the squished PB&J sandwich that her mom had made for her. "First I saw Jonathan, and then I bumped into Melissa, who was having a major picture-frame crisis and was pretty upset."

"So you were with Melissa Tait all this time?" Kara asked, her face tightening.

"Look, I know you don't like her. Especially after she took my djinn ring and bound me, but actually, she's not so bad. I promise."

"If you say so, then I believe you," Kara said as she used her finger to trace a pattern on the table. "It's just

I thought…well, it doesn't matter. So have you figured out a way to stop your mom going on a date yet?"

"No, but it's okay because Harvey reminded me that I just need to stay positive," Sophie said as she tried to figure out why Kara was acting so weirdly. Perhaps it was because she was nervous about going to the movies tomorrow with Patrick. *Patrick!* Sophie let out a long groan. "Oh, no. I was supposed to be trailing Patrick today to get an idea of what things you could talk to him about? I can't believe I forgot. Kara, I'm so sorry."

"Sophie, it's fine," Kara quickly assured her in her kindhearted way. I know you've had a lot on your plate. Especially with your mom and Mr. Rivers. Besides, I'm just being silly. I'm sure that I'll be able to talk to Patrick tomorrow. Plus, Harvey's been giving me some body-language tips, so even if I feel like throwing up, I can still make it look like I'm relaxed and having fun."

"Not to mention how to smile and nod her head if she gets tongue-tied," Harvey added. "It's a kind of 'fake it till you make it' approach."

"And don't forget that I'll be by your side the entire time at the movies," Sophie said, her cheeks still feeling flushed with guilt. Still, the important thing was that Kara seemed happy, which meant all Sophie needed to do was come up with a solution to stop her mom from dating Mr. Rivers, and everything would once again be perfect.

13

SOPHIE PUSHED ASIDE THE FLOOR PLANS THAT SHE was supposed to be studying and looked at the Kandinsky postcard again. It was a weird combination of bright colors and geometric shapes. Kara had tried to explain the theory behind it, but to Sophie it wasn't even artwork, it was a prison that was holding her dad captive.

It was so unfair. If only she could get him today. Like in twenty minutes. But even a positive thinker like her knew it was impossible. In fact, Sophie wasn't even sure she believed in positive thinking anymore; if it really worked, why was her mom still in her bedroom down the hall getting ready for her date?

Her date who was due to be here in twenty minutes.

Even for the Universe, this was cutting things pretty close.

Farther down the hallway, Sophie could hear Meg stomping around and fake coughing, no doubt to try to stop their mom from going. If Sophie thought that it had any chance of working, she would be fake coughing as well.

She put the postcard down and looked at her carpet, which was rolled up in the corner of the room. She had told Malik that she would practice doing some more parking maneuvers on it, but right now her heart didn't feel up to it. And had she mentioned just how unfair this all—

But the rest of her thoughts were lost as she caught sight of a puff of smoke, and a moment later, a fat orange djinn with a sea of necks and a large nose suddenly appeared in her room.

"Rufus, what are you doing here?" she yelped, her hand instinctively covering the Kandinsky postcard as Malik's words of caution rang out in her mind. Sophie bought a lot of things from Rufus's online djinn supply store, though his service didn't normally extend to making house calls. "A-are you looking for Malik?"

"I had hoped to find him," Rufus agreed in an unconvincing voice, which did nothing to ease Sophie's concern. He glanced around the bedroom with interest, and, as he paused to study her rolled-up carpet, Sophie took the opportunity to slip the Kandinsky photograph deep into the pocket of her jeans. If he knew she was looking for her father, he might start to wonder why she was looking for him.

"Sorry, he's not here." Sophie dredged up as much casual ease into her voice as she could muster.

"Oh." Rufus shrugged, looking far from disappointed as he pulled out a small gold and silver bag and handed it to her. "Well, I suppose it doesn't matter. It's just that he recently ordered some stabilizers for a flying carpet, which I assume were for you. Anyway, I figured that since they were for such a good customer, you might like this."

"W-what is it?" Sophie reluctantly took her hand out of her pocket to peer inside the bag.

"It's carpet wax. You rub it on, and it makes flying a lot smoother. Definitely handy if you get motion sickness. Oh, and don't worry. No charge for that."

"Thank you. That's very kind of you."

"It is, isn't it? But then again, I'm a djinn of exceptional generosity," Rufus agreed in a serene voice as he started to prowl the room, his numerous chins wobbling from the activity. Sophie wasn't a body-language expert like Harvey, but it was pretty obvious that Rufus didn't seem to be in a hurry to leave.

"S-so was there anything else?"

"Well…now that you mention it, there was one other small matter." He finally came to a halt and narrowed his eyes. "You see, I was at the camel races yesterday, and I bumped into an old acquaintance of mine. Karl is his name. Anyway, we got talking, as two old friends often do, and he told me the most extraordinary story. About how Malik cornered him and asked him numerous questions about Sheterum's mansion and where he could get the floor plans for it. Almost like he wanted to break in there, but of course, what djinn in his right mind would break into a sahir's mansion? After all, it's not like you could release anyone who was bound to Sheterum, and really, stealing from a sahir is never a good idea. So I guess I just wanted to check that Malik—whom I love like the juvenile delinquent brother I thankfully never had—wasn't in over his head."

"Oh." Sophie crossed her fingers and hoped that Rufus hadn't noticed the way her lips were uncontrollably twitching. "I'm really not sure w-why Malik was asking Karl those things. Perhaps you can discuss it with him when he comes back."

"I guess that's that then." The other djinn gave a casual shrug as he inspected his fingernails, which were incredibly well buffed. He finally looked up at her again. "Of course, then I remembered the rumors about how your dear father—and one of my very favorite customers—Tariq the Awesome was working on Sol... *well, I won't bore you with the details*...but I just wanted to say that if those rumors of what Tariq had been working on happened to be true, then you could have a very-sought-after commodity on your hands."

This time Sophie had to clamp down on her tongue to stop herself from yelping out in panic as Malik's words came back to haunt her about what would happen if anyone discovered that she had successfully made Solomon's Elixir. What would they do? Would they try and steal it from her? Or tell the Djinn Council? Just the thought of it made her shudder. She was so close to finding her dad—there was no way she was going to mess it up now.

Instead, she forced herself to give a casual shrug.

"I'm not really sure what you're talking about."

"Well, no matter then." Rufus finally stopped inspecting his nails and looked up, treating her to an engaging smile that did nothing to calm her nerves. "But for argument's sake, say that if you *were* successful in finishing off the work that your father had allegedly started, then it stands to reason that you would be looking for an A-plus distributor. Someone who would not only ensure that this *unique* product was marketed in the most beneficial way, but also offer you *very* reasonable returns."

Some of Sophie's panic left her as she rubbed her ears to check she had heard correctly. "R-right, so are you telling me that you're here to offer your services to me?"

"Why, of course, dear child. And while I know Malik dabbles with other retailers, let me assure you that in the djinn world, my reputation and my establishment are second to none. Well, apart from Seris and his knock-off emporium, but I've got it on very good authority that the Djinn Council will be taking his license away from him due to the small matter of unpaid back taxes. So if you were to need a business partner for any venture that you might or might not be pursuing, then I'm definitely a djinn you can rely on."

"I see," Sophie said as a sweet rush of relief went racing around her body. "Well, thank you for the offer. I'm just sorry that you came all this way for nothing."

"Meh. It's nice to get out of the office from time to

time." Rufus didn't seem unduly dismayed. "But if your situation were to change, remember that I—the djinn who gave you carpet wax for absolutely no charge—would love to be of assistance to you."

"Okay." Sophie obediently nodded and let out a sigh of relief as Rufus held his fingers high above his head. However, before he could disappear, the door was thrust open, and Meg came charging into her bedroom, her blonde ringlets flying in all directions and a look of annoyance plastered onto her small face.

Sophie immediately jumped to her feet in alarm, uncertain whether to be more concerned about the fact that an overweight orange djinn was in the room, or that there was a magical flying carpet rolled up in the corner. Thankfully, Meg didn't seem to notice either, and Sophie shot Rufus a grateful smile as she realized he must've made himself invisible to humans. Definitely one less thing to worry about, but Sophie didn't like taking chances. She hurried over to Meg.

"Hello, privacy. How many times do I have to tell you not to come barging into my bedroom like that?" she demanded as she put her hands on her sister's shoulders and steered her back toward the door. The moment she did, Sophie immediately wished for the large carpet to once again be underneath her bed, while wincing at the impact the wish had on her. *That was way too close.* Not to mention the fact that Rufus was still in the room, a curious expression plastered all over his round face. Sophie gulped as Meg continued to hover just outside the doorway. "Anyway, what do you want?"

"The sitter's here, and Mom said that Mr. Rivers was coming in ten minutes," Meg said in a dark voice as she simultaneously folded her arms and stomped her feet, while showing no intention of leaving. "You promised."

"Look, this might sound crazy, but I just *know* that Mom won't go on the date tonight. You've just got to trust me, okay?"

Meg paused for a moment to consider it before finally nodding her head. "Fine, but if you muck it up, then I swear that I'll put beetles in your bed for a week." Without another word, her sister stalked back to her bedroom, and Sophie shut the door and rubbed her brow.

"Date? Ouch. That sucks, so I guess she's moved on from Tariq the Awesome? I wonder if it's because he's bound to Sheterum? I mean, some women just don't find that an attractive quality in a partner. It's like they lose their alpha appeal or something," Rufus mused, causing Sophie to stiffen in annoyance. The moment she did so, the door pushed open, and Mr. Jaws poked his head through.

"She hasn't moved on," Sophie retorted as Mr. Jaws wove his way over to where Rufus was standing. "It's just that she doesn't know about my dad and what's happened to him, and it's not like I can exactly tell her the truth."

"Good point. I forgot how funny some mortals are about djinns," Rufus agreed as Mr. Jaws now started to rub his body against Rufus's leg. Then the next thing

Sophie knew, the cat had rolled onto his back so that his belly was exposed. *And was he purring?*

Sophie paused for a minute and widened her eyes, but Rufus merely grinned as he laboriously knelt down to pat Mr. Jaws. "Don't look so surprised—cats love me. And actually, that's another factor to remember if you were ever to need my services. *Rufus: loved by cats everywhere.* Catchy, no?"

"Er, if you say so. Anyway, if you don't mind, I've got a lot of stuff to do."

"So I gather." Rufus awkwardly stood back up, his numerous chins wobbling from the effort. "And just out of curiosity, what kind of wish are you going to use on your mom to stop the date tonight?"

"What do you mean?" Sophie, who was in the process of trying to shoo Mr. Jaws out of her room, forgot all about the cat and turned to Rufus with interest. "I can only conjure up inanimate objects. I can't do any behavior modifications—which is pretty annoying since, if I could, the first one I'd use it on is Mr. Jaws. Anyway, I was just going to do some more affirmations and trust the Universe to come up with something."

Rufus made a choking noise. "The Universe? Well, no offense, but I would rather put my faith in a reverse-image wish than in a random and immeasurable source that may or may not exist. But hey, that's just me."

"What's a reverse-image wish?" Sophie was immediately intrigued.

"A reverse-image wish is when a person looks into someone else's eyes and sees her worst nightmare come true. Of course, it can't be anything that isn't in the person's true nature to begin with. For example, say if someone loves stinky blue cheese and your mom hates it, she will immediately see that he or she is a stinky blue cheese eater. So basically, if there's anything your mom hates that this date dude does, she'll see it. There's a slight hitch in that if your mom and this guy are meant to be together, then all she'll see is happiness."

"They're not," Sophie replied firmly before shooting Rufus a questioning glance. "Which means that this sounds perfect. I just don't understand why Malik didn't tell me about it? According to him, I don't have enough power for any of the really good wishes."

"Well, grudgingly, I must admit that Malik's right. As a noob, you're simply not powerful enough to handle a spell like this. *However*," Rufus quickly added, obviously noticing the confused expression that was morphing across Sophie's face, "he was obviously forgetting all about my brand-new Rufus's Reverse-Image Tonic. Now, I don't like to boast, but it truly is amazing, and all you need to do is sprinkle a few drops on your mom's date and then wish for her worst nightmare to be revealed. The date will instantly turn into whatever kind of slobby, blue-hockey-shirt-wearing, leaves-the-toilet-seat-up guy she wants to avoid. And as a generous gesture to demonstrate my goodwill, I would be more than happy to give you a bottle at absolutely no charge. Not even postage. Or handling. In fact, let me get you a bottle right now."

Before Sophie could even open her mouth there was a rustle of feathers, and the now familiar-looking pink pigeon appeared in the room. Mr. Jaws immediately disappeared out the door, but the bird hardly noticed as it deposited a lavish silver gift bag into Rufus's hand and then vanished again in a flurry of feathers.

"So you're really certain that all I need to do is sprinkle it onto Mr. Rivers, and it'll work?" Sophie asked to make sure, since if there was one thing that Malik had taught her, it was that you could never be too careful about trusting other djinns.

"That's correct." Rufus nodded his head as he handed over the gift bag. "And once again, please let me remind you that there is absolutely *no* charge for this item. Not even for the stylish gift wrapping."

But Sophie hardly heard him as she pulled away layers of silver wrapping and took out a slim bottle. Then she grinned as she let out a little prayer of gratitude. She just knew the Universe would find a way to make it work.

14

"OKAY, SO ON THE WHOLE I THINK I LIKED YOUR other plan better," Harvey announced five minutes later from the other end of the phone. Sophie had tried to call Kara, but there was no answer, so she'd rung Harvey to let him know what had happened.

"What are you talking about? I didn't have another plan," Sophie reminded him.

"Exactly." Sophie could almost see Harvey nodding his head in agreement from the other end of the line. "And I definitely thought that was better. I mean, are you seriously telling me that you're going to wait until Mr. Rivers comes to pick up your mom and then turn invisible so you can sprinkle him with some special tonic to make your mom see her worst nightmare?"

"I know. It's inspired, right?" Sophie grinned.

"Only if you're a crazy person. What if he turns into a giant slug monster or something?" Harvey countered. "And what does Malik say about this?"

"I've got no idea. I haven't seen Malik since this morning. And for the record, there are no such things as giant slug monsters," Sophie reminded him as she tucked the handset under one ear so she could tie her favorite sneakers. "And on the plus side, if Malik isn't here, then he won't be able to complain when I give you a ride on the carpet when you get back from your weekend away with your mom," she added in a cajoling voice.

"Yes, but... *what*?" Harvey suddenly sounded torn between his normal worrywart persona and his desire to get on the carpet. "You'll give me a ride? Really?"

"Absolutely. I'm going to be practicing all weekend, so by the time you're back, I'm sure that I'll be ready to go out on my own." Sophie grinned a victory smile as she wriggled her toes and stood up.

"That does sound pretty awesome," Harvey admitted, just as there was a loud crashing noise on the other end of the line.

"What was that?" Sophie asked, jumping in surprise.

"Oh, my mom's ticked off that my dad didn't wash my gym clothes, and now she has to do it; she's taking out her anger on the trash can," Harvey said with a long sigh. "Anyway, I guess I'd better go. She wants to drive by my dad's apartment and tell him that he owes her five bucks for some laundry detergent before we head out to Camp Just-Kill-Me-Now."

"Harvey, that stinks. Are you okay?"

"You mean apart from the heartburn it's giving me? Yeah, I'm okay," he said, just as there was another crashing noise in the background. "That's my cue to go, but I'll see you on Sunday when I get back from what is going to be the lousiest weekend ever. And tell Kara not to freak out tomorrow. You know I'm the worrier of the group, and I say she'll be fine."

"I'll tell her," Sophie promised as she finished the call. Now all she had to do was sneak outside and wait until Mr. Rivers arrived so she could sprinkle the stuff on him and make the wish. Then, when she knew it had worked, she could sneak back upstairs to her room like nothing had happened—you know, just like a regular Friday night at home.

She was just congratulating herself on such an amazing plan when her mom poked her head through the door. She was wearing the red dress she had bought at the mall the other day as well as lipstick, mascara, and the faintest hint of perfume. She also looked exactly how she used to look before their dad had left them. Sophie's throat tightened.

"Okay, so Meg's watching a shark DVD in her room and Mrs. Corbett's downstairs," her mom said as she nervously smoothed down the soft fabric of her dress.

"Great." Sophie rolled her eyes as her mom walked farther into the room and glanced around, as if somehow knowing that there was an invisible flying carpet rolled up under the bed.

"Honey, I know this whole date thing is hard for you, but I'm hoping it will get easier in time."

*Doubtful,* Sophie wanted to say, but to her surprise before she could, she felt hot tears prick in the corner of her eyes. She hastily rubbed them away and commanded herself to stop being so stupid. The date wasn't going to happen anyway, and soon her dad would be home and everything would be back to the way it was supposed to be. Crying was just dumb. However she wasn't quick enough and her mom's mouth slipped into a disappointed frown.

"Sophie, if you're doing this to get me to change my mind—"

"I'm not." Sophie quickly turned away, pleased that she had a backup plan because if crying *had* been her plan, she would've been in big trouble. Then she realized that she needed to sneak outside before Mr. Rivers actually arrived so that her mom could see the truth immediately. She randomly picked up her Spanish books. "Anyway, if that's everything, I'd better get back to my homework."

"Okay, then. I'll go back downstairs and wait for Max." Her mom looked slightly surprised, but instead of saying anything else she gave Sophie a final smile and disappeared back out of the room. Sophie waited until she was gone before she grabbed the bottle of tonic from behind the computer monitor, where she had hidden it, and slipped it into the back pocket of her jeans. Then she turned herself invisible.

She made her way to the mirror to check that it had worked. No reflection stared back at her, and once again she marveled at just how cool being a djinn could be. She wondered if this was how Malik felt when he came and went as he wanted. It was certainly a liberating feeling, and once she had freed her dad, she would definitely have to start having some more fun with it.

But right now she had a job to do, and so she silently made her way down the stairs. Her mom was sitting upright on one of the hard dining room chairs, tapping her foot and glancing at her watch.

Even though her mom couldn't see her, she could still hear her, and Sophie was just trying to figure out how to get past the squeaky floorboard when Mr. Jaws decided to see just how far up the curtain he could jump. Sophie made a mental note to treat him with an extra bowl of Pretty Kitty snacks to thank him for the distraction. Her mom immediately went and detached him from the dark velvet drapes, giving Sophie the perfect chance to slip out the back door. From outside she could hear the faint echoes of Meg's shark DVD, but she ignored it as she stealthily made her way around to the side of the house to wait for Mr. Rivers to arrive.

The cool fall air nipped at her skin, and her teeth were starting to chatter as she stomped her feet to keep out the chill. Apart from all the other reasons why this date was a bad idea, it seemed like Mr. Rivers was late, too.

Finally, a sleek red Alfa Romeo pulled up. Sophie scrambled to her feet as she watched Mr. Rivers get out of the car. She opened the bottle that Rufus had given her and carefully took out the eyedropper, and she watched her mother's date pause a moment on the top step to re-arrange his tweed jacket and smell his breath by blowing into his hand. Ewh. The sooner this fiasco was over with, the better. Sophie made her way over to him, careful not to make a noise.

Rufus had said that four to five drops would be enough, and she was just squirting the last one onto him when he suddenly stepped forward and rang the doorbell. The surprise caused Sophie to jump, and the eyedropper al-most went flying from her hand, but she quickly steadied herself and shook off the couple of drops that had acci-dently squirted onto her own finger. Then she put one final drop onto the back of his ugly tweed jacket before closing her eyes and making the wish.

*I wish my mom would see the truth about Mr. Rivers.*

An intense shudder rippled through her like an earth-quake, and Sophie knew without a doubt that the wish had worked. She could feel it still buzzing and tingling through her veins like soda, and—

The rest of her thoughts were cut off as her mom an-swered the door. Sophie immediately caught her breath and leaned forward so that she wouldn't miss anything.

"Max, you're—" her mom started to say before a look of confusion spread out across her face and she rubbed her eyes as if trying to clear her vision.

"Louise?" Mr. Rivers asked in an uncertain voice. "Are you okay? You look like you've seen a ghost."

"I…actually, no, I don't think I am okay," her mom

stammered in a shaky voice before she nodded for him to come inside the house. Sophie took the opportunity to slip in as well, because if her teeth chattered any louder, she was pretty sure her cover would be blown.

"Can I get you something? Some water? An aspirin?" Mr. Rivers asked, his confusion giving way to concern. But Sophie's mom just shook her head and sat down in the closest chair while Mr. Jaws, who had been sleeping by the stairs, suddenly leaped up and padded over.

"No, it's nothing like that," her mom said as the cat jumped into her lap. She absently started to pat his fur as she took a deep breath. "This is going to sound terrible, but I've suddenly realized that I can't go out with you tonight."

Wow! Sophie widened her eyes in excitement. Of course she'd had complete confidence that the wish would work, but she hadn't expected it to work quite so quickly. She edged closer to her mom to see what she had seen when she looked at Mr. Rivers's face. But to Sophie he looked just the same as he always did. Salt-and-pepper hair. Blue eyes. A slightly crooked nose. But whatever her mom had seen had obviously done the trick. Ten bucks said it was some nose picking.

"It's the tweed jacket, isn't it?" Mr. Rivers let out a long groan as he obviously tried to figure it out, too. "I knew it was too old-fashioned, but—"

"No." Her mom managed a watery smile. "No, the jacket is fine. I actually like the tweed. The thing is you've been such a good friend to me, and I thought . . . well, I hoped that maybe in time I could—"

"Make yourself like me?" Mr. Rivers finished off with a rueful smile. "I had kind of hoped that, too."

"Except when I opened up the door and saw you standing there, it just made me realize that the only man I ever want to see on the doorstep is my husband," her mom said, sniffing and shaking her head. "It's so stupid. I mean, it's been four years. You would think I'd be over it by now. Max, I'm so sorry."

Mr. Rivers immediately shook his head. "Louise, you don't need to be sorry. The heart wants what the heart wants. And if your heart just wants to be friends with me, well, that's okay."

"Good friends," her mom said, and shot him a wobbly smile. "And thank you for being so understanding. W-would you like to stay for some coffee? I just need to cancel the sitter."

"A good friend might stay, but a better friend can see that you probably need to be on your own," he said with a patient smile. He turned and headed for the front door. "If you ever change your mind, then—"

"I know. And thank you." Her mom nodded as she followed him to the front door and walked him down the path. But Sophie didn't bother to go with them. All she knew was that it had worked. It had really worked.

15

"YOU MISSED A SPOT," MALIK ANNOUNCED THE following morning just as Sophie finished wiping the toast crumbs off the chopping board. She immediately dropped the dishcloth and spun around in surprise to see him floating near the kitchen ceiling. He was wearing a new-looking Hawaiian shirt and some purple trousers that would've looked awful on anyone else, but on him they just looked like…well…*Malik*.

"You're back," she yelped in surprise before remembering that talking to Malik out loud in the middle of the house probably wasn't such a smart idea. Thankfully, since it was Saturday, her mom was sleeping in, and Meg was outside talking to Jessica Dalton over the back fence. But all the same, Sophie didn't want to risk their walking in. She nodded for him to follow her back upstairs. He paused long enough to grab the uneaten toast that Sophie had just made, then he obediently followed her, leaving a trail of crumbs. Once they were in the safety of her room, she shut the door and turned to him.

"Where have you been? And if you say you were gal-livanting in Paris again, I will kill you."

"Kill me? Hello, you're the one who keeps pointing out that I'm already dead." Malik finished off the toast in one final bite and floated down to the ground. "And I'm sorry that I didn't come back last night. I just couldn't face see-ing your mom with *that man*. Still, it's not like they can get married or anything, so I suppose I shouldn't take it so badly."

"Especially since she didn't go on the date." Sophie beamed, unable to stay mad at him when everything was going so well.

"Really?" Malik immediately brightened. "Let me guess? She found out about the nose picking?"

"Actually, she found out that she still loved my dad," Sophie said, unable to stop smiling. "With a little help from me, of course. I did this amazing wish. It was a reverse-image wish so that when my mom first saw Mr. Rivers, her—"

"Whoa. Go back for a moment. Did you just say reverse-image wish?" Malik's face drained of color.

"That's right. It's this really great wish that—"

"Reveals a person's worst nightmare, blah, blah, blah," Malik finished off. "Yeah, I know what it is, but please in the name of all things shiny, tell me that you didn't use one. I mean, what sort of scumbag person would even think of selling you that?"

"W-what do you mean?" Sophie looked at him in alarm.

"I mean that reverse-image wishes are highly unstable, and over the years they have been related to numerous disasters, which is why they are so seldom used anymore. Also, they should especially never be used by minors."

"But Rufus never said anything about that," Sophie said as her heart began to pound in her chest and she searched through her drawer to find the small bottle. "He said it was fine."

"Rufus? You bought it from Rufus?" Malik instantly grabbed the bottle from her and studied the label before looking up at her in horror. "Sophie, after everything I've taught you, why would you buy something like this from him?"

"In my defense I didn't buy it. He gave it to me," she said, rubbing her brow and trying not to freak out. "I think he wanted to impress me in case I really had managed to create Solomon's Elixir. He's got it in his head that I should let him distribute it for me."

"Oh, this is not good." Malik started to fly around the room, his normally smooth Zac-like brow etched with worry lines. "Not good at all. I mean, using one of Rufus's tonics is always a risk, but even more so when you're already using an invisibility patch, anything could've happened to you. What were you thinking?"

"I was thinking that I didn't want my mom to go on a date before my dad comes home," Sophie reminded him before realizing that he was really bothered. "Besides, it worked *perfectly*. I turned invisible, put the tonic on him, and then listened to my mom call off the date. The moment she saw him she knew that she couldn't go through with it. It was amazing. And as for Rufus, I totally convinced him that I didn't know what he was talking about."

"Well, I still don't like it." Malik finally stopped floating around the room and crossed his arms. "I mean, this is Rufus we're talking about, and let's just say that when it comes to making tonics, he doesn't exactly have a stellar reputation. I remember this one batch of hair-growing liquid that he made for those djinns who were a bit concerned about their receding hairlines. Next thing you know, they all looked like yetis. The only reason he didn't lose his license over that little fiasco was because one of the old dragons on the Djinn Council actually had a thing for yetis and she thought it was cute."

"And I think that you're a bit too jaded," Sophie replied with a shrug as she held out her arms to demonstrate. "I mean, do I look hairy? His tonic worked perfectly, I promise."

"Humph." Malik made a muttering noise, which Sophie ignored as she stood up and grabbed her favorite purse.

"Anyway, I've got to go. I said I'd get to Kara's house early so we could have a last-minute jewelry consultation before we go to the movie."

"And that's another thing," said Malik, still in his petulant mood. "I don't think you should be gallivanting off to a movie when you're meant to be practicing your carpet flying. Not to mention the fact that I'm starving, and I need you to conjure me up some food since I'm guessing your mom's cooking hasn't improved since I've been away."

"Sorry, but we'll have to practice this afternoon. Kara's been completely frantic about this movie all week. There's no way I can bail on her," Sophie said, moving toward the door. "But I'll get you some food as long as you absolutely promise not to cause any trouble. Especially since my mom's probably still feeling a bit weird about the whole Mr. Rivers thing."

"Me? Cause trouble?" Malik blinked, and Sophie rolled her eyes before she wished for two Big Macs and fries. A second later Malik launched himself at them like he hadn't eaten for a month—or even like he was an actual person who needed food instead of being a dead djinn.

"Just promise me," Sophie said.

"I promise," he assured her with a mouthful of fries. Then he looked at her with interest. "Don't you think you should make yourself un-invisible before you go to Kara's house? In my experience humans tend to get a bit freaked out when they open the door and no one's there. Of course, sometimes it's funny, but if Kara's still wound up about this movie business, then maybe it's best not to spook her?"

"What?" Sophie paused for a moment and stared at him. "Is this some kind of weird trick to make me stay in and practice?"

"Er, no. I mean, if I was going to do a trick on you, I can assure you it would be a *little* bit more sophisticated than the old 'Wait, you're invisible' line." He gave a disdainful snort as he stuffed some more fries into his mouth.

"Yes, but I'm *not* invisible," Sophie retorted as she looked at her arm for proof.

"Have you looked in the mirror recently?" Malik demanded as he nodded toward the large wall mirror that was hanging next to her prized Neanderthal Joe poster. "Because I think you'll find that you are most definitely—"

"What?" Sophie stared in the mirror at her complete lack of reflection. She spun back around and looked at Malik in alarm. "How can I be invisible? I mean, I haven't so much as snapped my fingers all morning. In fact, the last time I was invisible was when I put the tonic on Mr. Rivers."

"You mean that completely harmless tonic that Rufus-the-least-trustworthy-djinn in the *whole entire world* gave to you?" Malik asked. "At least tell me that you didn't touch any of it."

"Of course not," Sophie assured him. Then an unpleasant memory of when several drops landed on her hand snaked into her mind. "Okay, so I touched it a little bit. B-but it was hardly anything. You can't possibly be telling me that I've been invisible since last night and no one's noticed."

"How should I know? Did you speak to your mom or sister last night? Or look in a mirror?"

"No to looking in a mirror, but yes to talking to my mom and Meg," Sophie said, and rubbed her chin. "Well, I think I… *actually, maybe I didn't.* After the whole 'dumping Mr. Rivers' thing, Mom just knocked on the door and said she wasn't going out but was going to have a hot bath and an early night. As for Meg, she didn't come near me," Sophie said, and a small sliver of panic started to churn in the pit of her stomach.

She quickly snapped her fingers and muttered the word visible. Then she stared at herself in the mirror, but there was still no reflection. Sophie took a deep breath and tried to ignore the fact that her hands were shaking. The important thing was that she didn't panic. She needed to stay calm and think positive thoughts.

"So"—she turned to Malik—"we just need to talk to Rufus and get him to fix this, right?"

"Have we learned *nothing* from what has just happened?" Malik stared at her. "Trusting Rufus is a bad, bad idea. Asking Rufus to help you fix the problem that he caused in the first place is an even worse idea. In a nutshell, Rufus and tonics do not go together. *Ever.* I'm not saying that he did this on purpose, nor am I saying that he doesn't have the ability to make things even more disastrous."

"Fine, so Rufus can't help us," Sophie reluctantly agreed as she shot him a hopeful look. "But there must be something we can do. How long will this last?"

"Well…" He paused for a moment as if to consider the

question fully before he finally looked up and shot her an apologetic look. "The worst-case scenario is probably a thousand years."

"A thousand years?" Sophie yelped in disbelief as her idea of not panicking went flying out the window. She used her hands to fan her hot, invisible face before she turned back to Malik. "I can't be invisible for a thousand years. I can't be invisible for even a day. I'm eleven years old. My mom will kill me. Plus, as a positive thinker, I've got lots of life plans already prepared, and none of them include being invisible. This is crazy."

"Hey, don't look at me. I'm not the one who used a dubious potion. Plus, I was only giving you the worst-case scenario. It's more likely that it will only last five or six hours."

"W-hat?" Sophie felt her jaw drop as she stared at him in disbelief. "And you didn't think to mention this alternative first?"

"I just thought it would make you appreciate how serious it *could've* been," Malik said, not looking remotely guilty. Though she couldn't help but notice that he put his arms protectively around his Big Macs. "And see, it worked. I bet you won't be taking any more strange tonics from Rufus again. So now that you're not going to see that movie, we should really get to work."

"Kara," Sophie yelped as she looked at her watch. "I'm late. I've got to go. I know it's not ideal that I'm invisible, but at least I can still talk to her and hold her hand. And actually, it might be better at the movies. Unless of course someone tries to sit in my seat. Hmmm, that could be a problem."

"Yes, why do you think that I hover so often?" Malik asked. "Of course, your other problem is that Kara won't be able to hear you," he added as an afterthought. "I might've forgotten to mention that."

Sophie stared at him in alarm. "Are you serious? No one can hear me? How can you tell?"

"You live long enough, you pick these things up. Plus, that revolting cat has been standing at the door for the last five minutes glaring at me, but it hasn't so much as blinked in your direction."

Sophie spun around and discovered it was true. Mr. Jaws was sitting low to the ground, his dark eyes fixed firmly on Malik. She hurried over and knelt down beside him, something that normally would've made the cat go all *Exorcist*, but instead he didn't even blink.

She hurried out into the hallway. "Mom? Meg?" she yelled at the top of her voice, but there was no answer, and she reluctantly went back into her bedroom and took a deep breath. "Okay, so this is not good. Kara is going to kill me."

"Sorry." Malik shot her an apologetic look. "Though if it's any consolation, you definitely get used to it. Plus, it's only for a few hours."

"You don't understand." Sophie shook her head in despair. "I promised her that I'd be there for her. Okay, there's only one thing to do. You're going to have to go in my place."

"What? You want me to go to the movies with a bunch of kids? Er, no thanks." He shuddered.

"You have to. You need to explain to Kara what's happened and just keep an eye on her. I know she'll be fine, but still, a promise is a promise. Besides," she added in a cajoling voice, "remember that it's *The Wizard of Oz*, and—"

However the rest of her words were lost as Malik suddenly snapped his fingers and disappeared from sight. *Well, that was Kara sorted out.* Now all Sophie needed to do was hurry downstairs and leave a note to remind her mom that she was going to Kara's for the day and then pretend to leave the house, before really heading back up to her bedroom and waiting for the whole invisible thing to wear off. Why did she get the feeling it was going to be a long day?

16

SOPHIE HADN'T BEEN KIDDING WHEN SHE HAD thought it was going to be the longest day ever. The good news was that her mom hadn't seemed remotely bothered when she'd seen Sophie's note reminding her that she was going to be at the movies with Kara. The even better news was that she had *totally* busted Meg sneaking into her bedroom and snooping through her stuff. Sophie had no idea what she was looking for, but she was still going to pay for it later. Just because her sister was only six didn't mean she shouldn't respect personal space— especially when that personal space was full of magic books and overpriced ingredients from Rufus's Bazaar.

However, now it was almost three in the afternoon, and despite checking the mirror approximately every thirty seconds, she was still completely invisible. She let out a sigh and turned her attention back to the flying-carpet book she had been studying.

Not that she was a fan of homework, but if they were going to go to Sheterum's mansion next week, Sophie wanted to make sure she was prepared. She was just going over the best way to avoid turbulence when she heard a scraping noise from over by her window.

She stiffened. She was sure it wasn't Malik because he wasn't a fan of nature. Ditto for Mr. Jaws, who preferred to save all of his climbing for the furniture. Which—

There it was again. Sophie grabbed the silver box that her dad had given her (which, as well as containing the recipe for Solomon's Elixir, was actually pretty heavy and therefore perfect for hitting someone on the head with). Then she clutched it to her chest and cautiously made her way toward the window.

Her heart pounded in anticipation. What if it was an intruder? She lifted the box high above her head just as the window sash eased open, but before she could bring it down, she recognized a familiar-looking sneaker. It belonged to Harvey. So did the leg that was attached to the shoe. Sophie immediately lowered the box as she watched her friend climb in through the window.

"Harvey Trenton. Don't you ever scare me like that again," she yelped as she tried to recover her poise.

"Sophie?" Harvey looked around the room in confusion as he awkwardly untangled his long legs. "Why can I hear you but not see you?"

"You can hear me?" Sophie blinked in excitement as

she dropped the box onto the bed and rushed over to the mirror. Unfortunately, there was still no sign of her reflection, but, still, the fact that he could hear her was a definite improvement of things.

"Well, yeah. Why? What's going on?" He pushed his long bangs back off his forehead and looked even more worried than normal.

"I could ask you the same thing," Sophie said as she still tried to get over the shock of seeing him at the window. "Since when do you climb into second-story windows?"

"Since I called your mom and she told me that you were at Kara's," Harvey retorted. "Besides, just because I don't always do guy things doesn't mean that I can't do guy things. It was actually pretty easy. Your mom might want to think about moving the trellis. It's almost like a stepladder. Anyway, the reason I'm here is to find out what the heck's going on."

Sophie let out a long groan as she nodded for him to sit down, then remembered that he couldn't see her. "You've got no idea how crazy things have been. The good news is that my plan to put that tonic on Mr. Rivers to stop him from dating my mom totally worked. Unfortunately, the bad news is that—"

"Let me guess. It made you invisible."

"That's right," Sophie said in surprise. "Have you seen Malik? Did he tell you?"

"Er, no. I'm just guessing from the fact that I can hear

you but I can't see you. Plus, this isn't the first time that your djinn magic has backfired," he said, looking at her in concern. *Well, he was actually looking at the dresser, but Sophie didn't have the heart to tell him that she was sitting cross-legged on her bed.* "So what happened? How long are you going to be stuck like this?"

"Malik thought it would wear off—oh, about two hours ago—but the fact you can hear me means that it hopefully won't be too much longer. Oh, and we need to be quiet because my mom thinks that I'm over at Kara's house. I said that we were going to hang out after the movie. That's why she told you I wasn't here."

"I know, but it doesn't tell me why Kara's mom totally refused to let me in the house just then. My mom decided that Camp Just Kill Me Now was full of loonies and crazy people, and so we stayed there for only half a day before turning right back around and coming home. Anyway, I thought I'd surprise you guys and see how the movies went, but instead Kara's mom gave me the total 'not on my watch' treatment. It was weird. So then I tried to text K, but she didn't reply, which was when I called you. By then my worry meter was on full alert, and I decided to climb up to see what I could find out. I was actually ex-pecting Malik to be here, not you."

"And that's what you would've found if only I hadn't managed to turn myself invisible." Sophie let out a long groan. "I mean, at least you can hear me now, but this morning it was nothing. That's why I sent Malik along to explain what had happened and to make sure she was okay."

"And have you seen him?" Harvey wanted to know as he walked over to the bed and sat down. Sophie just managed to scramble out of the way before he squished her. Did she mention that she was totally over this whole invisible thing?

"No—" she started to say. Before she could finish there was a rustling noise in the corner, and Malik suddenly appeared. "You're back," she squealed as she shot him a hopeful look. "So how did it go? Was Kara okay?"

"Okay, so the good news is that I love that movie. I mean, did Judy have some great shoes or did she have some great sh—?" Malik asked before Harvey cut him off.

"What about Kara? She didn't lose the power of speech or anything when she was with Patrick, did she?"

Malik winced. "Okay, as it goes, there is some bad news, but before I tell you, can I please just remind you that I'm a two-thousand-year-old djinn. A dead djinn. I'm really not equipped to handle these sorts of situations."

"W-what sorts of situations?" Harvey asked in a cautious voice. "What happened?"

"Remember how she had problems speaking around Patrick?" he asked, and when Sophie and Harvey both nodded their heads, he let out a sigh. "Well, this time she had problems shutting up. It was like a river, and I swear I heard words like *bedazzle* and *Barbie doll*s, not to mention her telling him about the time she had forgotten to wear underpants in first grade."

"Oh, no." Sophie let out a strangled groan, but Malik held up his hand to silence her.

"Trust me, it gets worse."

"Worse than the no-underpants story?" Harvey shuddered.

"I'm afraid so. You see there was also a Fanta/popcorn incident, and honestly I'm not even sure how it was physically possible, but somehow Kara managed to tar and feather her date with her snack bar items. In front of the entire drama club."

"So what happened then? What did she do?" Harvey asked in a hoarse voice, and Malik shrugged.

"She did the only thing she could do. She ran out of the movie theater and went home. I tried to stop her by telling the story of how I embarrassed myself in front of Cleopatra, who then refused *ever* to set eyes on me again, but for some reason that just made her more upset."

A sickening sensation burned in Sophie's stomach. Poor Kara. She had been so worried about this date, and, as it turned out, she had good reason to worry. A cold chill rushed through her as she got to her feet.

"I have to speak to her."

"She's not answering her phone, and her mom won't let anyone in," Harvey reminded her, but Sophie just shook her head as she raced over to where the carpet was rolled up. For a moment Harvey blinked, probably because to him it was invisible. However, Malik could see it perfectly well, and he narrowed his eyes.

"Sophie, what are you doing?"

"I'm going to Kara's," she said in a determined voice. "I need to tell her how sorry I am. Besides, you know as well as I do that I need the practice. I can visualize Kara's bedroom almost as well as my own. Please, Malik, don't try to stop me."

For a moment Malik looked torn, then finally nodded. "Fine. But I want you to come straight back here afterward. No joyriding."

"What about me? Can I go?" Harvey asked eagerly as he realized what was happening. But Malik shook his head. "Not this time, big guy. When Sophie's moved off the stabilizers and can do a three-point turn without falling off, then you'll get your chance."

"Thanks, Malik," Sophie said as she quickly spread out the carpet onto her bedroom floor. Once it was smoothed down, she crossed her legs and went through everything that Malik had taught her. First she cleared her mind, and then she created a bubble around herself before visualizing Kara's bedroom and blinking three times.

Next thing she knew, there was a tug in her stomach, and when she opened her eyes she was sitting on Kara's floor, looking up at where her friend was sitting cross-legged on her bed. Kara's long hair was hanging like a curtain over her face, and there was a sketch pad in her lap, but it was her red-rimmed eyes that made Sophie feel the worst. Without saying a word, Kara dropped her head and began to sketch.

"Kara, I'm so sorry. I feel terrible that I wasn't there," Sophie said in a rush, but instead of looking up, Kara just kept on sketching. "Please, K," Sophie tried again. "Could you stop drawing for just a moment so I could talk to you? I know how bad you must be feeling, but you've got to try to let it go. It wasn't your fault."

Kara suddenly looked up, her normally pale green eyes seeming somehow much darker. Almost like wood. "I know it wasn't my fault."

"Oh," Sophie said in surprise. "Well, that's good. I mean, it's all about having a positive attitude."

"Actually, it's all about figuring out who my friends really are, because as far as I'm concerned, this was your fault."

"What?" Sophie blinked. "Look, I really do feel bad about that, but you've got to know that I'd never do anything bad to you on purpose. Oh my gosh, Malik did tell you I was invisible, right? And that besides not being able to see me, no one could hear me, either?" Sophie suddenly asked, knowing that when it came to details, Malik wasn't always the most reliable.

"Yes, I know all about that. But can't you see? You only got turned invisible because you didn't want your mom to go on a date with Mr. Rivers, so you used your magic. You even used your magic to help Melissa Tait and her picture frames. But what about me? I needed you to be there with me. I didn't even want your magic; I just needed you to remind me that no one should *ever* hear the story of how I forgot to wear panties in the first grade. But you weren't, Sophie. You weren't there when I needed you."

Sophie widened her eyes in confusion. She had expected her friend to be mad, but she hadn't expected this. "Kara, I'm—"

"No. Sorry isn't going to cut it this time." Kara gave a firm shake of her long dark hair as she thrust the sketch into Sophie's hand and then stood up and marched to the door. "I'm going downstairs, and when I come back up, I want you to be gone."

"But—" Sophie tried to add, but it was too late. Kara was gone. Sophie stared at the sketch, her stomach churning with distress. She was no expert, but she was fairly sure it wasn't a good sign that Kara had drawn a detail-perfect portrait of Sophie, and then had ruthlessly scribbled it back out with long dark gashes that must've caused the lead in her pencil to break. And underneath was written the word: *Selfish.*

Sophie felt ill as she made her way back to the carpet and crossed her legs so that she could leave. The moment she reappeared in her bedroom Malik and Harvey practically pounced on her.

"So?" Harvey demanded. "What happened? Is it all okay now?"

"No." Sophie stretched her legs out and studied her sneakers. "It went badly. And by badly I mean *badly*."

"So she's still annoyed about the whole Fanta/popcorn thing?" Malik winced. "I was worried about that. Especially since the soda fell in what most bros would consider a very undesirable place for soda to fall."

Sophie groaned. "What am I going to do? I tried apologizing, but she totally won't listen. It's like she thinks that I wanted this to happen. Why would I want my best friend to humiliate herself in front of her crush? It doesn't make sense."

"Welcome to my world," Malik said as he chewed on a stray Cheeto that he plucked up from the desk. "None of what you and your friends do makes sense to me."

"Yes, well, if you *really* want to see something that doesn't make sense, then check this out," Sophie said as she waved the sketch in Malik's direction. "I mean, look. She scribbled out my face *and* called me selfish. Why would she do that?"

"Well," Malik said as he wrinkled his nose. "Though, if I'm being completely honest, you are a *little* bit selfish sometimes."

"Exactly," Sophie started to agree before realizing what he'd just said. "Excuse me, but *what?* How am I selfish? Why would you say that? I'm always conjuring you up food. And for Harvey and Kara as well."

"All the time," Harvey agreed, but Malik, who was now floating above her, folded his arms.

"I know you are. But here's the thing. Right now you've had so many big, important, crazy changes in your world that you probably haven't really noticed what's been going on in everyone else's world."

"I-I haven't?" Sophie stammered as her throat tightened up. "Like what?"

"Okay, but first, please don't get mad at this because I'm on your side, remember? And I'm not just saying that because I want you to give me a positive evaluation for the Djinn Council—though if you feel I was worthy of full marks, then please don't let me stop you. Anyway, I digress, my point is that lately you keep talking about how awesome and amazing it's going to be when your father gets home. Like all the great things we're going to do."

"What's wrong with that?" Sophie asked as she tried to ignore the way her lower lip was beginning to quiver. "I was just being positive. It really helps to visualize."

"I know, and it's wonderful, but the thing is you're forgetting that I won't be here. Your father is one of the greatest djinns who ever existed—apart, of course, from the small whoopsy of getting himself bound—you won't need me as a djinn guide anymore."

"Malik…I don't know what to say." Sophie stared at him as she realized he was right. She hadn't remotely thought any of this through. "I just assumed you would still be here. I—"

"Look, it's okay. I know it was an accident, but I'm just using this as an example. For you it was important to stop your mom from going on her date with *that man*. But for Kara—"

"It was important that her best friend was at the movies with her to stop her from pouring Fanta all over her crush's crotch," Sophie finished off as she reached out and studied the scribbled-out sketch. Then she felt a wave of nausea rush over her. What had she done?

17

I T WASN'T MEANT TO BE LIKE THIS. SOPHIE WAS
supposed to be happy that in under an hour she and
Malik would be flying to rescue her dad. After all, this is
what she had wanted for four years. But any excitement
she felt was tempered by the fact that despite a week of
apologizing, Kara still wasn't speaking to her. In fact,
not speaking didn't really do the situation justice. Kara
also wasn't looking at her, breathing near her, or even
acknowledging Sophie's existence.

It probably didn't help that someone at the drama club
had posted a YouTube clip of Kara's embarrassing moment, and while it wasn't exactly getting a million hits,
it was certainly popular with all the students at Robert
Robertson Middle School.

Sophie glanced over to the ornamental boulder where
Harvey and Kara were both standing, deep in discussion.
Part of Sophie longed to click her fingers and say the word
*invisible* so that she could find out how it was going. The
only thing stopping her was that she knew that if she was

caught, then Kara would be madder than ever. So instead, she was forced to wait to see if Harvey had any success. As she watched them, she pulled out the list of things she had tried to do to convince Kara of how sorry she was.

It included talking to Patrick to remind him how lovely Kara was and how she had embarrassed herself in front of her entire Spanish class just to draw the attention away from her friend. Not to mention all the e-mails, instant messages, and phone calls. But none of it had worked.

Sophie took a deep breath to stop the tears from falling and was just deciding if she should forget about it and call her mom to pick her up when she caught sight of Jonathan and Melissa walking toward her. Despite the gloom of the last five days, Sophie felt herself returning his infectious smile as Jonathan made his way over.

"Hey." His grin faded as he caught sight of Kara and Harvey over by the boulder, and he furrowed his brow. "Why aren't you waiting over there with your friends?"

"Keep up, brother dear," Melissa said, looking as perfectly groomed as ever in a pink polo and some impossibly trendy earrings. "Sophie's friend Kara was giving her the look of death yesterday. It was vicious. I like that in a person."

Jonathan shot Sophie an apologetic grimace. "And once again, please ignore my sister. My parents assure me that we're related, but I'm still looking for evidence."

"Try the mirror," Melissa retorted, then gave an unrepentant shrug and turned to Sophie. "Besides, it's not like it's going to last. I've got no idea what the deal is, but I bet that your friend Kara folds in a day."

Somehow Sophie doubted it. "I hope so. Anyway, how are the party plans for Sunday coming along?"

"Superbly," Melissa answered before Jonathan could even open his mouth. He rolled his eyes.

"My parents hired a very expensive planner to do it, but Melissa has kind of hijacked the whole thing in her quiet and unassuming way."

"Yes, well, if it was left to those idiots, we would have a string quartet and bits of bread with asparagus on them. Sushi, people. Why haven't you heard of sushi? Oh, and that reminds me, I need to make a new list. Sophie, do you have a pen I could borrow?"

"Sure." Sophie bit back a smile as she realized that Melissa's abrasive personality was actually quite funny. She opened her backpack and was looking for her pencil case when Melissa suddenly leaned over and plucked out a piece of paper that was near the top.

She winced as she realized it was the sketch Kara had done. The one where she had scribbled out Sophie's face. Sophie had planned to throw it away, since she was sure that nothing positive could come from it, but she couldn't quite bring herself to do it. Especially since, as the week had progressed, Sophie had realized that Kara had been right. Sophie was a bad friend, and the picture was a way of reminding her just how bad she had been.

"Oh, this is interesting," Melissa said without a flicker

of sarcasm as she studied it intently. "There's some nice energy and flow going on in this. Did you draw it?"

"I can barely do stick figures." Sophie shook her head, her throat once again tightening up at the venom in her friend's sketch. "It was Kara. And that's why I know that she isn't going to get over this fight anytime soon."

"Man, that's brutal." Jonathan shuddered as he gave Sophie an apologetic smile. "Sorry, I didn't mean to make you feel worse, but she must be really mad at you."

"I know." Sophie sighed. Part of her longed to tell Jonathan what had really happened, but then that would involve mentioning wishes going wrong, being a djinn, and the fact that she was a bad friend.

"Seriously, you two are a great match because you're both equally dumb." Melissa looked up from the picture and shot them both a disgusted look.

"Huh?" Sophie blinked while Jonathan narrowed his eyes and did some kind of unspoken twin thing to Melissa. Whatever it was that he did seemed to do the job, and Melissa let out a pained sigh.

"Okay, so what *I meant to say* was that if your friend did this drawing, it's not because she hates you and wants to scribble you out, it's because she's mad at herself. She's trying to scribble out her own work. So whatever her problem is, all you need to do is fix it, and you'll be all warm and fuzzy once again."

"What? How do you know all this?" Sophie asked in surprise.

"Because my mom owns an art gallery. Because how can I run a fashion and lifestyle empire when I'm older if I don't have a basic understanding of art. And finally, because I'm a lot smarter than most people give me credit for. Now, as much as I'd love to stand around talking to you both about how clueless you are when it comes to art, I need to make sure that the caterer has enough glasses."

"Sorry, she's a bit stressed about Sunday," Jonathan apologized before looking at his watch and giving her a rueful grin. "Anyway, I'd better go and help her, but I'll try to IM you tomorrow, and I'll see you at the party. And try not to get too freaked out about Kara. Melissa's scary smart when she puts her mind to it, and our parents have been dragging us to galleries for years. Personally, it all looks like squiggle to me, but she seems to get it, and so if she says it means something, then there's a good chance she's right."

"Thanks, I really hope so," Sophie said just as she realized Harvey was slowly jogging toward her. She gave Jonathan a final smile and took a deep breath as Harvey reached her.

"So what did she say?" Sophie nervously clutched at the sketch in her hands, while trying not to glance over to the boulder, where Kara was still standing.

"I'm sorry, Sophie." Harvey sighed and studied the ground.

"But she must have said something," Sophie insisted, her voice going squeaky with panic. He glumly shook his head so much that his long bangs went flying back and forth like windshield wipers.

"She made me promise not to tell you."

"What? But that's not fair. How am I supposed to fix this when she won't let me talk to her, and now she won't let me even talk to you?"

"She's not stopping us from talking; she doesn't want us to talk about her," Harvey clarified. "I tried to tell her that open conversation was a lot healthier, but—"

"Look, I know that this isn't your fault, but can you at least tell her how sorry I am? And maybe ask if there is *anything* I can do to make it up to her. I mean, nothing I've tried has worked. What should I do?"

"I'm sorry, Soph." Harvey dropped his head again, and his long bangs now covered his eyes. "I wish I knew. She's really mad. The thing is that I can't stay in the middle any longer. You guys are my best friends, and I'm already stuck in the middle of my folks and their endless arguing. I can't have it with you guys, too."

Sophie's chest immediately tightened, and she had to clamp on her lip to stop from crying. "Harvey. I'm so sorry. I don't want you to get stressed."

"Too late. Do you think it's possible to die of heartburn at the age of eleven?"

"I think the cafeteria meat loaf will kill you before the heartburn does," Sophie reassured him in a light voice that was the total opposite of how she was feeling.

"So what do we do now? Kara wants me to get a lift

home with her, but that will mean you're on the bus on your own. Plus"—he broke off for a moment and let out a long breath—"well, I wanted to help you get ready for D-day."

Sophie wanted him to as well. It was bad enough that Kara wasn't going to be with her, but now Harvey? She could feel the tears creep up into her eyes, but she forced them back as she glanced over to where Kara was still standing. She didn't look happy or smug. She just looked sad. Sophie took a deep breath and shook her head.

"You should totally go with K. I've already been a horrible friend to her. I don't want to make it any worse by taking you away. Plus, Malik should be at home waiting for me, and my mom is taking Meg to some shark lecture at the museum, so she won't even know that I'm gone."

Harvey still looked torn, and despite not being a body-language expert like he was, Sophie could see that he was upset. "Okay, but Sophie, please be careful. This is serious stuff, so don't do anything stupid. Promise me."

"I promise," she said in a small voice. "Besides, Malik turned into some kind of alter-ego drill sergeant, so we've gone over everything loads of times." It was ironic actually; because Kara wasn't talking to her and Harvey was spending only half as much time with her, Sophie had been doing a lot of practice. She no longer panicked when she saw an oncoming floor polisher, and they'd been over the security details of Sheterum's mansion so many times that she almost felt like she'd already been there.

"Okay, well, make sure you call me the minute you get home."

"I will," she promised just as the bus pulled up. Then she watched as Harvey jogged back to where Kara was standing, and they both turned and started walking over to the second parking lot, where they were meeting Kara's mom. It looked like Melissa Tait was wrong after all. Kara was never going to talk to her again. And the worst thing was that Sophie couldn't even blame her. She had been selfish, and now she was paying the price. It was just that she had no idea it would make her feel so bad.

18

BY FOUR O'CLOCK THEY WERE READY. SOPHIE shook with relief since she was fairly certain that her frayed nerves couldn't handle any more waiting. Malik had made her go over every single detail a hundred more times, and, whatever dumb fantasy she'd had that Kara and Harvey might turn up was gone. She was on her own. Well, she still had Malik, but soon he would be gone, too.

Sophie took a deep breath and began to unroll the carpet onto her bedroom floor. Once that was done she wrapped her fingers around the small vial of Solomon's Elixir and said a silent prayer to the Universe, asking for it to be on her side.

"Hey?" Malik looked up from where he had been pouring over the floor plan one last time. "Are you worried about landing the carpet in the right spot? Maybe I shouldn't have told you about the laser beams and how they pulverize your brain if they touch you. We've been practicing all week, and you've totally nailed those landings. I'm ninety-nine percent sure that we're ready for this."

"I'm okay," Sophie quickly assured him as she slipped the elixir into her pocket and went over everything in her head one more time. According to what Manny had told Malik, the guards tended to do their paperwork twenty minutes before they finished their shift, which meant they didn't monitor the security screens as carefully as they should. It was the only window of opportunity they would get.

However, that wasn't the only obstacle. In the room was a series of laser beams laid out like a 3D grid that Sophie would have to land in. According to Malik, she could simply use her magic to wish them away, but in doing so she would trigger the alarm system, and they would then have only one minute before the guards arrived. Which meant that once Sophie did deactivate them, she would have to pour the elixir on the painting, release her dad, and get out of there in under a minute.

No pressure then.

At least, unlike her hopeless attempts at trying to convince Kara she was sorry, all the practices had gone really well. According to Malik, she was as ready as she was ever going to be.

"Okay, so it's time. Let's do this thing," Malik announced as he smoothed down the bright blue harem pants he had chosen for the occasion; they were clashing violently with his Wildcats basketball shirt and made him look more like a Vanilla Ice wannabe than a two-thousand-year-old ghost. He had tried to convince Sophie that since this was her first big mission she should wear something similar, but she opted for her jeans and her favorite Neanderthal Joe T-shirt instead, as well as her Eddie Henry guitar pick.

"I'm ready," Sophie assured him and glanced at her watch. "So it's four o'clock, and hopefully my mom won't be back until five. If she finds out that I've been gone, I'll be grounded for the rest of my immortal life."

For a moment Sophie thought of Kara, but she quickly pushed the thought from her mind. This was it. What she had been dreaming of for so long—not just seeing her dad, but bringing him home so they could be a family once again. It was for her. For her mom and for Meg. And that's why she knew that she could do it.

She walked over to the carpet and sat on it in a cross-legged position. Malik joined her, and Sophie suddenly felt her throat tighten as she turned to him. Yes, most of the time he was a complete pain in the butt who got her into more trouble than he was worth. Not to mention the fact that he constantly forgot to tell her vital bits of information. But...but all the same, she was going to miss him like crazy when he was gone. She closed her eyes for a moment and felt a familiar tingle go racing through her.

"Hey." He grinned in surprise. "Cheetos. What are these for?"

"I've heard it's the universal language for 'thank you,'" Sophie said. "I guess I just wanted to—"

"What? Okay, whoa. Stop right there." Malik put up his hand and looked at her in alarm. "The first rule of being a djinn is never to make soppy and emotional speeches. Especially not to dead djinns who tear up far too easily and in turn can wind up in embarrassing and undignified moments," he added, and shot her a rueful smile. "And besides, it's not like I'm dead. Well, okay, I'm totally dead, but I can still come to visit. All you have to do is clap your hands and summon me."

"Malik, you *never* come when I clap my hands and summon you," Sophie reminded him with a watery sniff.

"Well, that's true, but I *will* visit. Especially if the Djinn Council hires me to do another training job and then sends me somewhere that doesn't have broadband or cable," he said in a light voice. But Sophie couldn't help but notice that he quickly busied himself with opening up the bag of Cheetos and avoided making eye contact.

"Thank you." Sophie shot him one last smile before she closed her eyes and concentrated on everything that he had been teaching her for the last two weeks. Then she slowly lifted her head, causing the carpet below her to rise gently off the ground. Once it was floating high enough, Sophie took a deep breath and prepared to blink her eyes. If she did this right, she would be in the long gallery in the heart of Sheterum's mansion, hovering directly in front of the painting her father was in. If she did it wrong...well...she was a positive thinker, so she wasn't about to go there. Instead, she loosened her grip on the sides of the carpet like Malik had taught her, blinked her eyes, and felt a familiar lurching of her stomach.

A moment later the disembodied feeling of being dropped from a great height left her, and Sophie cautiously opened her eyes. Malik had warned her to lean forward when she blinked, and she had assumed this was to give herself a smoother landing. But she now realized that it was because the grid work of thin red laser beams was so tight.

As she glanced around from her hunched-forward position, she realized just how close they really were. One sneeze would be enough to bring on the brain pulverizing. Once she calmed down, she awkwardly pulled the Solomon's Elixir from her pocket to make sure it was still safe. It was, but that didn't stop the adrenaline from pumping through her veins as she studied the room.

It was a long gallery, exactly like the picture Manny had given them, with impossibly shiny polished wooden floors and ornate plaster cornices. She could also see hundreds of tiny laser-thin red lines that sliced through the room, making it look like something out of a Tom Cruise movie. But the one thing that wasn't there was the Kandinsky painting. The wall she was looking at was completely bare.

Next to her, Malik was looking equally alarmed as he hunched forward, clutching at his harem pants so the voluminous fabric wouldn't hit any of the beams that were caging them in.

"What happened?" Sophie tried to crane her head around, but it was difficult when they were so restricted. "Do you think Manny tricked us?"

"No." Malik started to shake his head before catching sight of a laser and obviously thinking better of it. "I have excellent radar when it comes to lying, cheating scoundrels, and I can always tell when they are fibbing. Plus, I totally gave him my favorite Zac Efron T-shirt."

"So where's my dad then?" Tears stung her eyes. "Do you think that Sheterum took the painting with him to Paris?"

"Again, no. Even if Sheterum took your father, the painting would still be here. Which means...oh—" Malik suddenly broke off and flattened himself farther down onto the carpet.

"What? Why did you just say 'oh'?" Sophie demanded. "Did you see some guards?"

"No, not yet. But look, we're facing the wrong way around." Malik used his eyes to indicate the door at the far end of the gallery. "That's where the guards will come in from, which means that the painting is behind us."

*What?* Sophie battled with the desire to scream. But screaming wouldn't help anyone, and it would most definitely alert the guards. So she forced herself to assess the situation silently. She had about five inches to her front, back, and sides but only one inch before her head hit a beam, which would make turning around very difficult. However, just as she realized that, Malik suddenly disappeared and then reappeared facing the other way.

Okay, well, it wasn't difficult for him, but it was going to be difficult for her. And according to her watch, she'd already wasted a minute.

"Sophie," Malik said, but Sophie cut him off.

"I know." She carefully twisted her torso while not lifting her head. Then she put her right hand out behind so that she could uncross her legs without losing her balance. If she had been playing a game of Twister, she would probably have fallen over by now, but this was no game. Sweat gathered on her brow as she began the awkward task of swiveling around without lifting her head or shoulders any higher.

"Sophie," Malik said again as she clamped down on her lip and edged her way around.

"It's okay, Malik. I've got this," she said with more conviction than she felt. As she moved, she tried not to look at just how close the red beams were to her face. Never had she been more grateful in her life that her flat hair didn't have any bounce in it. Instead, she continued to twist herself around until she was finally facing the other way, lying forward on her knees like she was about to do a push-up. "See. I told you that I could—"

But the rest of her words were lost as she realized what Malik had been trying to tell her. Horror rose up in her throat, its icy fingers tightening their grip as she stared at the wall. There wasn't just one Kandinsky painting; there were thirty of them. All identical and all staring back at her. Sophie's heart hammered in fear as her grip around the Solomon's Elixir vial tightened. What was she going to do now?

19

"OKAY, SO THE IMPORTANT THING IS NOT TO PANIC," Sophie counseled herself as she tried to ignore the grim expression plastered on Malik's normally relaxed face. Instead, she continued to stare at the wall, her eyes a blur of color and crazy geometric shapes all swirling and taunting her. "I mean, there's obviously a logical explanation for why there are so many copies of the same painting."

"They're not the same." Malik's voice was serious and did nothing to alleviate Sophie's growing fear. "They are all subtly different, and they're all there because sahirs are cunning evil creatures who love to play tricks. Unfortunately, this is one trick that we didn't count on. I don't suppose you brought your copy of the original painting, did you?"

"No," Sophie gulped. "I didn't even think of it, but if it's any consolation, I can tell you exactly where it is in my sock drawer. Do we have time to go back to get it?" she asked as they both continued to sit perfectly still in their awkward positions, trapped by the lasers.

"No." Malik's expression was grim, and Sophie felt her heart begin to pound in her chest. "I know you found the trip easy this time, but it's actually very draining, which is why we didn't practice doing locations farther away before. By the time we get back, you'll need at least twenty-four hours to recuperate, and Sheterum will be back by then."

"W-what about wishing for it to appear?" Sophie asked, but Malik just dropped his voice lower.

"I'm sorry. Manny gave us the codes to teleport in here without being detected, but if we use any more magic, we'll leave a magical residue and trigger the alarm."

Sophie felt the color leach from her skin. "S-so what *can* we do?"

"We can try like crazy to remember what the original painting looked like because we only get one shot at this, and if we get it wrong . . ." Malik let his voice trail off, but Sophie didn't need him to finish the sentence to know that this was very bad indeed. Especially since she had been so busy learning how to fly the carpet and studying the floor plans that she had barely given the painting itself a second thought. Something that she was now bitterly regretting.

She stared at the thirty paintings on the wall, each of them calling out "Pick me, pick me" to her. But she couldn't do it. Her dad was stuck in one of those paintings, and it was up to her to unbind him. But if she picked the wrong painting, then it would all be for nothing.

She would've failed, and she might never have another chance. She had to pick the right painting. Why hadn't she studied the photograph better? Why hadn't she taken a picture of it and put it on her cell phone? Oh, yes, that's right, it was because she didn't have a cell phone and—

"That's it!" she suddenly said, still leaning forward so that she wouldn't accidently hit the lasers. "I can call Harvey and ask him to climb in through my bedroom window and check the postcard. It wouldn't be the first time he's done it."

"Sophie, even if you told Harvey that the postcard was covered in nachos and lasagna, he wouldn't be able to get there in time," Malik said with a groan, still hunched forward on the carpet. "This is all my fault. I'm a bad djinn guide. The worst. I mean, this is a classic sahir trick, and I fell for it."

"Don't be silly. Of course you didn't think of it, because what djinn in his right mind would go into a sahir's mansion? But we don't have time for this right now. We need to get this figured out, so even if Harvey can't get to my house in time, he can still look it up on the Internet. Kara said it was a totally famous painting before Sheterum stole it. Can I use your cell phone?"

For a moment Malik blinked and then grinned. "I was wondering when the old Sophie would come back." He awkwardly managed to wriggle his cell phone from out of his harem pants and passed it over. Sophie propped herself up on her elbows so that her hands were free. First she took photographs of all the paintings, and then she scrolled through for Harvey's number.

"Soph?" Harvey immediately answered. "Are you back? What happened? Is everything—"

"Okay, short version is that we're stuck in a laser-beam grid staring at thirty copies of the same painting, and since the alarm will be triggered when I deactivate the lasers, I've only got one shot at doing this. If I send some photographs of all the paintings to you, do you think you could look the real one up on the Internet and figure out which one it is? Oh, and the guards will be changing in ten minutes."

"Of course," Harvey immediately answered, not bothering to ask unnecessary questions, which made her feel overwhelmingly grateful.

"Thanks, H. I'm sending them now." She finished the call and let out a sigh of relief as she quickly sent him all the photographs. Then she turned to Malik and tried not to notice how pale his face was looking. Not that she could blame him, since there was no way of knowing if Harvey would even find the painting on the Internet, let alone figure out which one it—

But before she could even finish that thought, Malik's cell phone began to vibrate. Okay, there was quick and there was quick, and her chest pounded with worry as she answered it, still careful not to move.

"Harvey?" she demanded. "Is everything okay? Did you get the photograph?"

"He did," a crisp voice on the other end of the phone said, and Sophie froze.

"K-kara?"

"Look, I know you don't have much time, so here's the skinny. I know which painting your dad is in."

"You do?" Sophie all but yelled before catching Malik's pointed glare as he nodded at the door to remind her that even though they weren't under surveillance, they could still be heard if anyone happened to be walking past. She immediately lowered her voice. "A-are you sure? It's just there are thirty paintings, and if we screw it up—"

"Sophie, on the life of Colin the flying monkey, I'm sure," Kara quickly assured her. "It's the one in the middle row, third from the left. There's a really defined blue line running through the left-hand side of it, and the yellow triangle is a lot darker. All the others are just cheap prints that someone's painted over. When I looked at the copies on the computer, it's really easy to see the faint lines of the original print where they've missed a spot. They're pretty basic forgeries that would never get past even the dumbest art dealer. But I guess they're only there to confuse people."

Sophie looked up on the wall until she spotted the painting Kara had described. It immediately stood out from the others, and the more Sophie looked at it, the less she could believe that she hadn't noticed it sooner. Next to her Malik tapped his watch to remind her to be quick.

"Kara, I don't know what to say," she said as the words choked in her throat. "After everything that's happened, I don't deserve for you to—"

"Stop. Look, I admit that I was angry. Public humiliation does that to a person, but then Melissa Tait came over to where Harvey and I were waiting in the parking lot and wanted to talk to me."

"What?"

"I know, right. Anyway, she said that my artwork was excellent for an amateur, and she'd love to see more of it. Then she added that I should stop showing it to you because you were a knucklehead who could only interpret artwork on a literal level instead of seeing it as a projective statement."

"That does sound like Melissa," Sophie agreed, and wrinkled her nose. "So what does that mean?"

For a moment Kara was silent, and then let out a groan. "It means that she thinks I was projecting myself into the painting, and she's right. Deep down, I was being selfish, too. You shouldn't have to fix my inability to talk to Patrick—I should. Which is why I called him when I got home."

"No."

"Yes, and we had a perfectly fine conversation during which my head didn't explode. Not even once. He also told me that you had gone to see him to tell him how great I was."

"Well, that wasn't exactly a hard conversation to have," Sophie sniffed. "Since you are pretty great…so, does that mean that we're friends again?"

"Of course we are. But let's finish this conversation later. After you and your dad have come home. I know you can do it, Soph. Harvey does, too."

"Thanks," Sophie whispered as she finished the call and handed Malik his cell phone. She couldn't help but notice that he looked like he had something in his eye.

"What? I think it's this air-conditioning. It's playing havoc with my sinuses. Anyway, don't you have a djinn to unbind?"

"I do," Sophie agreed as she kept her eyes firmly on the painting Kara had told her was real. Then she wished that the red laser beams would disappear. A familiar tingling feeling went charging through her, and the laser beams were gone. A second later a piercing alarm shattered the silence.

It took all of Sophie's willpower not to bury her head in her hands to try to block out the noise. Thankfully, Malik had warned her that this would happen, and so Sophie gritted her teeth and wriggled back into a sitting position. Then she guided the carpet forward until they were sitting directly in front of the painting.

Next to her Malik stiffened, but strangely enough, after everything that Sophie had been through, she felt a sense of calmness wash over her. She wasn't sure if it was because of the Universe or because she had Kara and

Harvey watching her back, but suddenly she knew be-
yond a shadow of a doubt that she was ready. She lifted
the small vial of elixir and carefully unscrewed the lid.
Then, without hesitating, she threw it on the Kandinsky
and watched as the amber liquid shimmered and trickled
its way down the brightly colored painting.

For a moment nothing happened, and Sophie's heart
began to hammer with nerves as she looked at the empty
bottle in her hand. If she'd made a mistake, then—

But the rest of her thoughts were cut off as the doors at
the far end of the long gallery went flying open and three
gorilla-sized men piled into the room.

"Come on, Dad. We need to go," she whispered in a
low, urgent voice, but still there was nothing. She could
feel her pulse fluttering as the guards' shoes pounded
along the wooden floorboards. "Come on—"

"Sophie, look." Malik suddenly pointed back to the
Kandinsky, which was now swirling like a windmill.
Sophie tightened her grip on the empty vial as the painting suddenly ripped open and a man came tumbling out,
landing with a thud on the floor just in front of them.

The noise caused the oncoming guards to stop in confusion, and that was all the time that Malik needed to
disappear off the carpet and reappear over the crumpled
body. Sophie instantly lowered her chin and brought the
carpet plummeting to the ground. She ignored the impact as she joined Malik.

He was saying something in a language that Sophie

had never even heard before, but all of her attention was on the figure in front of her. He was skinnier than she remembered, and his face was pale and his breathing shallow. A wealth of emotions threatened to overwhelm her as she reached out and gently touched his face.

"Malik, it's my father. We've found him—"

"And if we don't want to lose him again, we need to get the heck out of here," Malik told her in a razor-sharp voice just as the guards snapped out of their confusion and raced toward them again. Without another thought she helped drag the motionless figure onto the carpet.

Then, just as the guards reached them, Sophie raised her head, causing the carpet to go shooting up toward the ceiling. Without even waiting for it to come to a halt, she blinked her eyes. The next thing she knew they were back in the bedroom of her house.

Sophie half expected to look up and discover that the guards had followed her, but instead, she saw only the familiar Neanderthal Joe posters and her incomplete Spanish homework.

"Dad. Dad. Are you okay?" Sophie immediately leaned over the prostrate figure, panic lacing her words. She turned to Malik in alarm. "He's not moving. What's wrong with him?"

"Probably the shock of that terrible landing," Malik retorted as he folded his arms and shot her a stern glare. "I would like to think that I taught you better than that."

"Um, hello. Did you not see the three big hairy guards

who were chasing us?" she protested, and then caught sight of her father's sunken cheeks and deathly pallor. "B-but what are you saying? Are we too late?"

However, Malik didn't answer. Instead, he nudged her out of the way and started once again to talk in the weird language. For a moment there was nothing, but eventually the low guttural sounds finally seemed to have an effect as her dad managed to open his deep navy eyes and glance around. He groggily edged himself into a sitting position, still looking disoriented.

Sophie let out a little gasp of joy as Malik suddenly faded back into the corner of the room. Then her dad turned to her and blinked as his gaze zoomed in on her face. She took in the familiar wild blond hair, the navy eyes that were the mirror of Meg's, and the three-day growth of beard that covered his chin.

"Sophie? Is that really you?" His voice was laden with confusion until he reached up and pulled her to him, enveloping her in a massive hug. Sophie let out a pent-up sob and crumpled into his chest as the last four years of worry came pouring out of her. The feel of his arms around hers, his familiar dad smell—it was all still the same. Exactly how she remembered.

She wasn't sure how long she was there before she finally pulled away and grinned.

"You're okay. You're really okay," she said, her voice still thick with tears.

"I-I think so," he said, his eyes never leaving hers.

"Though I have no idea what just happened. I was bound to Sheterum, I know that much. But nothing else makes sense. How did you find me, how did you get in to rescue me, and why do you look so much older than the last time I saw you?"

"It's kind of a long story," Sophie gulped. She suddenly appreciated why Malik had disappeared into the shadows. Then she took a deep breath and started to fill her dad in on what had happened during the last four years, her hand never leaving his.

Half an hour later her dad was still looking as if he had just stepped out of a wrecked car. "I've been gone for four years?"

"I'm afraid so," Sophie said. Malik had explained to her that time moved differently when you were bound, but she hadn't really understood what he'd meant until now. The drained expression on her dad's face really said it all.

"And while I was gone you managed to get turned into a djinn by someone called Malktrek," her dad continued, his grim face growing grimmer by the minute.

"His name is Malik. And I told you it was an accident. Plus," she added in a rush, "he's been a really big help since it happened, and there's no way I would've been able to rescue you without him."

"Hmmm, well, I think I'm going to need to meet this

Malik," her dad said in a menacing voice, and Sophie turned to where Malik was still lurking and nodded for him to come out.

"Er, Tariq. Hi," Malik said in a cautious voice as he floated into the light, a contrite expression on his normally jovial face. "About the whole 'tricking Sophie into taking my djinn ring' thing. I mean, obviously, I never would've done it if I'd had any idea she was your daughter. Not to mention—"

"Malik, enough." Her dad held up his hand. "I'm not going to pretend I'm happy about what's happened—"

"Dad," Sophie cut him off, "don't you dare get mad at him."

"Actually, Sophie, your father has every right to get mad at me." Malik shot her a gentle smile. "Especially since, if your father had wanted you to be a djinn, he would've registered you with the council when you were first born. But don't worry, Tariq, I promise that I'll leave immediately, and you have my word that I won't come back again."

"No." Sophie shook her head. "He can't go. It wasn't his fault, and besides, he's been a really amazing djinn guide. Not only did he help me with transcendental conjuring, but he was the best flying-carpet teacher that a girl could have."

"Did he tell you to say all of that?" her dad asked, his jaw still clenched.

"No, of course not—well, perhaps he made some suggestions for when I fill in his djinn guide evaluation—but you were the person who taught me to speak up for myself. So please, you can't get mad at him. I won't allow it."

"Sophie," Malik said in a soft voice, "it's okay, and I promise that I will come to visit you sometimes. Well, if that's okay by Tariq."

"Ah, now I remember you. A terrible poker player and quick to run out on a bad hand," her dad said as he folded his arms.

"Excuse me?" Malik looked surprised.

"You heard me. You're obviously the same in death as you were in immortal life. After all, what kind of djinn guide leaves his student after just eight weeks?"

Malik rubbed the bridge of his nose in confusion, but Sophie widened her eyes as she turned to her dad.

"Are you saying he can stay?" she gasped.

"Seriously?" Malik clapped his hands together but remembered that cool djinn guides didn't clap their hands, so he folded his arms instead.

Her dad let out a long sigh. "I'm pretty sure that I will probably regret it. A lot. But I also remember what a disaster it was when I tried to teach Sophie how to ride a bike when she was six."

"I crashed into the hedge and got a massive cut on my arm. Mom was mad at for you ages," Sophie recalled with delight, and her dad ruefully nodded his head.

"Pretty much. Besides, I'm going to need all the allies

I can get if I'm going to come out of this in one piece."

"Out of what?" Sophie asked in alarm as she immediately glanced around her bedroom. "What's going on? Are you still in trouble? Will Sheterum come after you? Malik didn't tell me that."

"No, don't worry, Sheterum won't come after me again, and if he does, he won't find it quite so easy the next time around. No, I'm talking about something else, and I'm afraid it's going to be a lot tougher than anything else you've been through so far."

"W-what is it?" Sophie gasped as her dad got to his feet and held out a hand to help her up.

"We need to go and explain this whole mess to your mom."

20

"GROUNDED?" KARA GASPED ON SUNDAY MORNING as they sat on the yellow-and-white comforter on Sophie's bed. "You saved your dad from a lifetime of being stuck in a painting and being at the beck and call of an evil sahir, and now you're grounded? That is *totally* unbelievable."

"I know, right?" Sophie waved her arms in outrage. "We had a family meeting that went on *all* day, and that's when Mom and Dad explained exactly why they were doing it. Apparently, it's because not only did I hide the whole djinn thing from my mom, but because I snuck out of the house. *To rescue my dad.*" Then she let out a sigh as she got to her feet and twirled around in the turquoise silk dress, admiring the way it made her short legs look super-long—well long for her. "Thankfully, they said it could start on Monday so that I could go to the Taits' anniversary party today."

"Speaking of which, are you sure that you don't mind if I come along?" Kara got to her feet and smoothed down the cute floral skirt that Sophie had originally planned to wear, and that, like everything Kara put on, looked amazing on her. "I got the shock of my life when Melissa called me up yesterday and invited me. She thought I might want to see her mom's David Hockney collection. I mean, hello, is she kidding me? Who wouldn't want to see it?"

"I told you she wasn't that bad." Sophie grinned as she clutched at the Eddie Henry guitar pick, which was hanging around her neck. "And she's even invited Harvey, too."

"Well, in between her snide comments, I guess she's okay," Kara reluctantly conceded just as Sophie's mom called for them to come downstairs if they wanted a lift to the party. The two girls grinned at each other as they hurried down to where everyone was waiting.

"I want to go, too," Meg said in a sulky voice. "It's not fair. First Sophie gets to be a djinn, and now she gets to go to the party?"

"Meg," their mom began in a sharp voice. But before she could say anything else, Malik appeared in a bright green Hawaiian shirt and some skinny jeans, an extra-large bag of Cheetos in his hand.

"And what about me? Why can't I go? I bet they're going to have some really great food there. Melissa Tait's very fierce and has a nice eye for detail. I was really looking forward to checking it all out," Malik said, earning him a sharp look from Mr. Jaws, whose opinion of Malik hadn't improved now that he could properly see him. And the cat wasn't the only one who could see Malik. It had been decided at yesterday's meeting that, if Malik was going to be around all the time, it was only fair if everyone could see him.

"Well tough luck, because neither of you is going," Sophie's dad said in a firm voice. "Malik, we've been through this. From now on if you want to live in this house, then you live by our rules, and that means no more Cheetos. They are not a food group. And Meg, I wouldn't be getting too jealous of your sister. As she's about to find out, being a djinn isn't all fun and games."

"What?" Kara widened her eyes and stared at Sophie. "What does that mean?"

"It means no more unauthorized magic," Sophie sighed, since that was the other major outcome of the family meeting that they'd had yesterday. And from now on she could do magic only in her lessons with Malik or if she had approval from her parents. Apparently, that even included tweaking her hair to give it more bounce, which, if you asked her, was more than a little unreasonable. Then there was the rest. Somehow she had forgotten that her dad was a planner, but as he ran down a twenty-five-point list, it all came flooding back.

"Sophie can't do any more magic?" Meg looked marginally happier.

"That's right," their dad said as he scooped Meg up

into a gigantic bear hug that soon had her giggling like a baby. "Anyway," he added, "after we drop Sophie and Kara at the party, your mom and I are going to take you to the aquarium to see the sharks."

"Really?" Meg squealed, the party instantly forgotten.

"Really, so you'd better go and get ready," her dad said with a grin. "And Malik, there's an apple pie in the kitchen. It's not quite as orange as Cheetos, but I think you might like it."

"And who exactly made this pie?" Malik asked in a cautious voice while inadvertently looking directly at Sophie's mom.

"Don't worry, it definitely wasn't me." Her mom didn't look remotely offended as she wrapped her arms around Sophie's dad, looking happier than she had looked in a long time.

"Well, in that case I'm in. No offense, of course," Malik hastily added.

"None taken, Malik. Or should I say MG?" Sophie's mom said as her lips twitched. Not only had she finally been able to see Malik for the first time yesterday, she had discovered that he was actually her Facebook friend MG, which, ironically enough, made her feel a lot more comfortable around him. Then she narrowed her eyes. "But Terry wasn't joking about living by our family rules. If you want to be part of this house, then I expect you to wash up your own dishes. Okay?"

"Dishes? Apple pie?" Malik said as he used his arms

like scales before finally shrugging. "Eh, I've heard of worse deals." Then he floated off to the kitchen, closely followed by an annoyed-looking Mr. Jaws. At the same time, Meg reappeared wearing her favorite shark-shaped sunglasses.

"Let's go already," Sophie's little sister commanded as they headed out the door and piled into the car that had miraculously turned from a ten-year-old Toyota into a brand-new Prius (thanks to her dad giving Rufus a call about distributing Solomon's Elixir for him). Personally, Sophie couldn't understand why her dad didn't just conjure up a new car, but he had explained that rule number one of being a djinn was that one didn't use one's powers for personal gain. At that point Malik had slunk off, pretending to answer a cell phone call.

The trip to Jonathan's house was mostly taken up with Meg bargaining for how long they could stay at the aquarium, but Sophie hardly heard. She was too busy enjoying the fact that she once again had a perfect family. Her mom, her dad, her sister. Even Malik and the petulant cat. Not to mention her friends, because she had quickly learned that life wasn't nearly as good when you didn't have your friends with you.

Finally, the car pulled to a halt and Kara got out, but before Sophie could, her mom twisted around from the front seat and handed her a large silver bag with mounds of tissue paper frothing over the top.

"What's this?" Sophie said in surprise as she took it.

"It's a gift for you to take to the party. Monica was admiring it the other day when she came to look at some stock, so I thought it would make a nice present for her anniversary," her mom said.

"Thanks, Mom!" Sophie said in delight; with everything that had been going on, she'd completely forgotten about a present. She carefully lifted out some of the tissue paper and gasped. It was one of her mom's pottery vases. This one was shaped like a twisted tree trunk and was glazed with a silvery paint that seemed to dribble down the sides. It looked almost haunted and ghostly, and Sophie was pretty sure that even Melissa Tait would approve. She looked at her mom and gave her a grateful smile. "Really, thanks, Mom. For everything."

"You're welcome, honey." Her mom gave her a watery smile and squeezed her hand. "You're still grounded, of course, but for today I want you to have a lovely time. Plus, you will need to take some notes. Your father and I have a wedding anniversary coming up next month, and let's just say that I intend on making up for the last four that we missed."

"A party?" Meg immediately clapped her hands. "Can we have a shark cake?"

"We'll see," her mom said, giving them a smile that Sophie hadn't seen in a long, long time. She let out a happy sigh and was just about to scramble out of the car when her dad stopped her.

"Actually, Soph, there's something I wanted to talk to

you about, too," he said, pausing and shutting his eyes. Then he opened them again, and Sophie realized that Meg wasn't moving. Instead, she was sitting with her mouth open, like she was just about to speak. Sophie widened her eyes and peered into the front seat, only to discover that her mom was also sitting perfectly still, like a statue.

"Um, Dad." She scratched her chin as she gave him a surprised glance. "Did you just freeze Mom and Meg?"

"Well, yeah," he reluctantly said before narrowing his eyes. "But this is one of the situations that falls under the 'Do as I say, not as I do' rule. Okay?"

"Okay," she agreed. "And if this is about the rules, then you don't have to worry. I promise that I won't forget any of them. No conjuring. No being invisible. No unauthorized carpet flying or listening to any rules that Malik tells me. I will be the model djinn."

"Actually"—her dad shook his head and gave her a goofy smile—"I think your mom and I have been so busy talking about your new djinn life that I forgot to talk about all the other things you've been doing."

Sophie looked at him in alarm. "Is this about the time I dropped chocolate ice cream on the carpet and pretended that Mr. Jaws did it, because I'm—"

"Honey, no," he quickly assured her and let out a groan. "I'm really bad at this parenting stuff. I think I'm going to need to do a catch-up course. Anyway, your mom told me what a positive thinker you are and how you always believed that I would come home, even when no one else did."

"Oh, well, that wasn't very hard," Sophie assured him in surprise. "Since I always just knew you would. It wasn't really difficult. Now, learning to fly the carpet. That was difficult."

"That's debatable. I know a lot of djinns who can fly, but not many who can remain so unfaltering in their beliefs. What I'm trying to say is, I'm grateful that your inner magic is just as strong as your outer magic," he said. "Anyway, we can keep talking about it later, but I just wanted you to know how proud I am of you and how happy I am to be home."

"I'm happy as well." Sophie shyly reached out and touched his shoulder, just to make sure he really was real. His hand reached up and squeezed hers, and for a moment they just sat there in silence.

"Okay, and now I will just turn into a boring dad if I don't let you get out of the car and go to your party. But, Soph, one more thing," he added before he closed his eyes. A moment later Sophie felt her hair begin to tingle, and she widened her eyes in surprise as she tentatively reached up and patted it. It was definitely more bouncy, just the way she liked it. Then her dad winked at her and her mom and Meg suddenly came back to life, just like nothing had happened. For a moment Sophie was silent, and she returned his grin. And then she hopped out of the car and hurried over to where Kara, Harvey, Jonathan, and Melissa were all waiting for her. The crazy thing was that all this time she had wanted her dad to come home so that their lives could go back to normal, but now she realized that there was no way that could happen.

From now on their life was going to be amazing.

Turn the page for a peek at the first book in the series...

# Sophie's MIXED-UP Magic

## Wishful Thinking

Amanda Ashby

BOOK 1

THERE WERE THREE THINGS THAT SOPHIE CAMPBELL knew to be true. First was that the power of positive thinking could make just about anything happen. Second was that Neanderthal Joe was the best band in the world and she didn't care how sold-out their concert was because she and her friends were somehow going to get tickets (see her above thoughts on positive thinking). And the third thing was that if Ryan the biter didn't let go of the brand-new jeans that she planned to wear tomorrow for the first day of sixth grade, then she was going to kill him. Kill him dead.

"I mean it, Ryan, hand them over now and no one will get hurt," Sophie said in what she hoped was a calm and collected manner.

"No." Ryan gave a simple shake of his red hair and wiped his face along one of the legs, causing Sophie to take a deep breath. So much for her calm and collected manner. Seriously, if any of the peanut butter from his face got onto her jeans, there was going to be trouble.

"Why's he doing that?" her best friend Kara wanted to know as she looked up from her sketch pad and wrinkled her brow in confusion. She had only just gotten back from her art camp yesterday and had decided to come along to keep Sophie company while she was babysitting.

"Because he's the devil," Sophie explained as she moved slightly to the left to block Ryan's path.

"Surely he can't be that bad. I mean, he's only six," Kara said in her typical kindhearted way as she put down her charcoal and joined Sophie over by the sofa. "Perhaps he's just playing a game?"

"Oh, it's no game. He really is the ultimate evil. I'm pretty sure I even saw horns," Sophie assured her as Ryan suddenly darted past them and through the open French doors that led out to the extensive garden. They bolted after him.

"Where did he go?" Kara joined her outside, blinking in the bright California sunshine as they both scanned the spacious grounds for any sign of him.

"I don't know. He could be anywhere." Sophie let out a frustrated wail while cursing herself for bringing her precious new jeans babysitting just so that she could show Kara how totally gorgeous they were. It was such a rookie mistake. Especially since every sitter in a three-mile radius knew what a nightmare Ryan was.

Ryan was actually the nephew of her mom's boss, Mr. Rivers, and the only reason Sophie had agreed to look after the little he-beast in the first place was because her mom had bribed Sophie with the brand-new jeans on the way over there.

Well, okay, there was one other reason that Sophie had agreed to do it, but she hadn't bothered to tell her mom about it (since she really had wanted those jeans without having to dip into her Neanderthal Joe savings fund). But the truth was that, in a happy twist of fate, Mr. Rivers lived next door to Jonathan Tait, who was one year older than Sophie and had a habit of practicing basketball in his backyard with no shirt on.

Unfortunately, despite being there for the last three hours, Sophie had seen neither hide nor hair of Jonathan, and even worse, her awesome new jeans were in jeopardy of meeting a gruesome death. All in all, not such a great day. Not to mention—

"There he is," she yelled as she suddenly caught sight of a flash of red hair speeding out from the side of the house before once again slipping past them. Sophie tried to ignore the way he let her jeans trail behind him on the ground. And was that a dirt mark she could see on them? *Oh, he was so dead.*

"Don't worry, Soph. We'll get them back," Kara said as they went racing back through the French doors, Sophie's favorite Vans making a soft padding sound along the hardwood floors. She took the stairs two at a time as Kara followed her. When they reached the top, she looked in both directions. There was no sign of Ryan anywhere, but she soon heard a high-pitched giggle coming from the guest room where he had been staying.

Sophie narrowed her eyes. She would high-pitch giggle him, she decided, as she went charging in there. Ryan was sitting on the large leather chair with his PS3 controls in his hands and an evil smirk on his freckled face. Unfortunately, her jeans were nowhere in sight.

"Where are they?" she asked in a tight voice as she peered under the bed. Kara appeared two seconds later and headed straight for the closet.

"Where are what?" Ryan mimicked in a way that made Sophie long to take his controller and use it to hit him over the head. *Stay calm and think happy thoughts,* she commanded herself. *You don't want to become known as the babysitter who murdered Ryan the biter.* Especially since, while she might not be the biggest fan of kids, she was definitely a fan of extra money, and if she killed Ryan, then she was pretty sure that her babysitting career would be over.

"My jeans, Ryan, where are my jeans?" she asked instead, with as much Zen-ness as she could muster.

"Can't remember." He giggled.

"Perhaps if I hang you upside down by your toenails it will help jog your memory?" she suggested.

"You're not allowed to do that; you're the babysitter," he reminded her, but Sophie just shrugged.

"Well, since I have no intention of ever looking after

you again, I don't really have much to lose. Now tell me: Where are my jeans?"

Ryan paused for a moment, obviously trying to decide if she was bluffing or not before he finally relented.

"Oh, right, *those* jeans. I put them down the laundry chute."

"You did what?" Sophie looked at him blankly since her own house wasn't quite big enough to have a laundry chute, and if she was honest, she wasn't even really sure what one was.

"I think he means that thing." Kara pointed to a small door in the wall, and Sophie felt her breath shorten as she immediately raced over and yanked it open. For a moment all she saw was pitch black as she stared down a long dark tunnel, but as her eyes started to adjust she finally caught sight of something blue lying in a crumpled heap down at the bottom.

Oh, thank goodness!

"I can see them and they're okay. I repeat, they're okay," she called out before spinning back round to where Ryan was still sitting. "So where exactly does this thing end up?" she demanded.

"In the basement, which means... *Hey, where are you going?*" Ryan widened his beady little eyes in surprise as Sophie grabbed Kara's hand and headed for the door.

"The moon. I've heard it's nice this time of year," she snapped in annoyance before tilting her head and glaring at him. "Where do you think I'm going? And you had better hope like crazy that they're not dirty."

"Yeah, well, you're not allowed down there, and if you go, I'll tell Uncle Max," Ryan said, making Sophie realize that he had totally done this on purpose, the little snot. Well, two could play at that game.

"Really, and perhaps I should tell your uncle Max what you did to his cat?" Sophie countered, since she had caught Ryan trying to water the one-eyed tabby earlier. And not in a nice way either.

"I was just playing with him." Ryan's voice started to turn whiny and sullen.

"And the big scratch you put in the back of the walnut desk downstairs?" Sophie arched an eyebrow. "Was that just playing as well? Because my mom works in your uncle's antique store, and I know for a fact that desk is worth over ten thousand dollars. I imagine he would be quite annoyed if he found out you'd ruined it."

"You w-wouldn't." Ryan faltered.

"Wouldn't I?" Sophie said as she shot him a double dose of her world-famous death glare. Okay, so it wasn't really world famous, but she had spent most of the summer practicing it in case Cheryl Lewis gave her any more problems in gym. She must've nailed it because Ryan instantly shut his mouth.

"Fine," he eventually muttered. "I won't say anything."

"Good. And I suggest that you stay here and play your

stupid game because otherwise I just might change my mind about what I tell your uncle Max. Now come on, Kara, let's go get my jeans."

"Wow, he really is evil," Kara said in awe as Sophie raced down the landing toward the wide staircase. "I can't believe he ruined a ten-thousand-dollar walnut desk."

"Actually, I don't have a clue how much the desk cost or what it's made out of," Sophie admitted with a rueful grin. "But I figured he's a six-year-old kid, so he wouldn't know either. The important thing is that it shut him up. Hopefully, he won't give us any more trouble."

"Well, you were very convincing," Kara assured her before suddenly pausing for a moment and frowning. "By the way, what did he mean about the basement?"

"Oh, that. Well, before Mr. Rivers left, he gave me a list of dos and don'ts, and one of them was that no one was allowed in the basement." Sophie shrugged as she reached the ground floor and headed toward the kitchen, where the basement stairs were.

"What?" Kara yelped as a flash of concern raced across her face. "Are you serious? He told you not to go in the basement, and you're still going to do it?"

Sophie, whose fingers were gripped around the basement door, wrinkled her nose. "Well, I can't really get my jeans back if I don't," she pointed out. "Anyway, it will only take a second."

"Yes, but it's a basement." Kara was looking seriously alarmed now. "You know what Harvey says. Going into the basement is the number one cause of death for young American girls. Especially when it's a basement that you've been warned not to go into."

"Kara," Sophie said, groaning. "Harvey was talking about horror-movie clichés—you know he watches far too many of those things. Besides, you don't seriously think I should leave my jeans down there, do you?"

Kara didn't reply, but Sophie could tell by the way her friend was chewing her lip that this was exactly what she did think. Great.

Most people who met Kara Simpson thought that while she was a little bit kooky, for the most part she was sweet and kind and wouldn't say boo to a ghost (though seriously, who in their right mind would say boo to a ghost in the first place? Unless, of course, you wanted to bug the ghost, and in that case you could boo away).

Not that that was the point. The point was that Kara had a stubborn streak that ran through her like a rod of iron. Two rods even. Normally it came out only when she was talking about postmodern art and its use of pop imagery, but occasionally it did make other appearances.

Now was obviously one of them.

Sophie's mom said it was because Kara was an Aquarius and therefore marched to the beat of her own drum, but all Sophie knew was that when her best friend chewed her lip like that, it was hard to change her mind.

"I have to go down there," she repeated in a wheedling voice. "They're my new jeans. *My new jeans that are going to look amazing on me when we start sixth grade tomorrow.* I can't just leave them there."

"Yes, but maybe you could just wait until Mr. Rivers comes home and ask him to get them then?" Kara suggested in a hopeful voice, but Sophie shook her head.

"He's away until later tonight. Ryan is getting picked up by his nanny, who is going to take him back to whatever planet he comes from. But she can't get here until later this afternoon, which is why they needed me to babysit in the first place."

"Well, you could always just wear your other jeans tomorrow. I mean they're cute, too."

They were also covered in pink embroidered flowers and made Sophie look about eight years old. Not exactly how she planned to start sixth grade. Besides, it was okay for Kara—with her long dark hair and her pale green eyes—because she could wear whatever she liked and still look amazing. But for Sophie, with her so-straight-you-could-rule-lines-with-it blonde hair and standard-issue brown eyes, it wasn't so easy.

For a start, she was four feet nothing (and judging from her gene pool, it didn't look like things would be improving anytime soon), so trying to find clothes that didn't make her look young, chubby, or, at the very worst, "cute as a button" was near impossible.

Not that she was complaining, she was just saying that when you weren't America's Next Top Model gorgeous like Kara, you needed to rely on other things to help you get by in life (or, to be more specific, to impress Jonathan Tait).

Hence, her beautiful new jeans, which felt like they were made especially for her. From the moment she had tried them on she just knew that good things would come from owning them. Plus, they somehow managed to make her look taller. Which was why she had no plans at all to leave them trapped on the other side of the basement door.

Those jeans were hers. Somehow the Universe had led her to them, and if she couldn't trust the Universe, then whom could she trust? Sophie felt her resolve strengthen as she twisted the door handle and turned and gave Kara a smile.

"Honestly, I'll be fine. I'll just go get my jeans, and then we can go back upstairs and you can show me the sketch you were doing."

"I don't know." Kara continued to bite her bottom lip in concern. "I still don't like it."

"Kara, relax. I mean, I'll be down there for two minutes tops. Seriously, what could possibly go wrong?"

J
FIC
Ashby

Ashby, Amanda.

Out of sight.

FRANKLIN SQUARE PUBLIC LIBRARY

| DATE | | | |
|---|---|---|---|
| | | | |
| | | | |
| | | | |
| | | | |
| | | | |
| | | | |
| | | | |
| | | | |
| | | | |
| | | | |
| | | | |
| | | | |

DISCARD

**FRANKLIN SQUARE PUBLIC LIBRARY**
**19 LINCOLN ROAD**
**FRANKLIN SQUARE, NY 11010**
**(516) 488-3444**

FEB    2013

BAKER & TAYLOR